"I owe you a lot, Skye."

"No, Bjorn," she protested uneasily as they walked along the white sand, the lake a quiet murmur in the still darkness. "You owe me nothing."

His fingers tightened on hers. "I do, you know. I never would have figured out why Karin resented me without your help." Bjorn put his hands on her shoulders and turned her to face him. He touched her lips softly with his. "Thank you," he said.

Skye closed her eyes momentarily at the jolt of sensation.

"I really love that girl, Skye," he added. "I'd do anything for her."

She squeezed his fingers in silent understanding. "I know." Her voice was soft. But where did she stand with him? she wondered. It was obvious he was grateful to her, but was that as deep as his feelings went?

SAMANTHA DAY, a Canadian author, used to work in a school library but now makes romance writing her full-time occupation. Having perfected the art of daydreaming, she says she learned how to transcribe what she saw in her mind onto sheets of blank paper. Her husband and daughter are wonderfully supportive and encouraging of her romance writing.

Books by Samantha Day

HARLEQUIN ROMANCE
2672—THE TURN OF THE TIDE

For Karin's Sake

Samantha Day

Harlequin Books

TORONTO • NEW YORK • LONDON
AMSTERDAM • PARIS • SYDNEY • HAMBURG
STOCKHOLM • ATHENS • TOKYO • MILAN

ISBN 0-373-02840-7

Harlequin Romance first edition June 1987

CHAPTER ONE

THE SOUTHERLY WINDS of morning reneged on their soft promise of spring. Pivoting suddenly, they shrieked once more from the north, hurling Arctic chill along the shores of Lake Winnipeg. Ice floes that had begun to disperse in the still, warming waters were turned in their paths and relentlessly thrust ashore in great grinding slabs.

Skye Cameron shivered and pressed her legs against the warmth of the big, shaggy black dog at her side. Excited by the clash of wind and ice, Skye absorbed the sight and sound of winter's futile battle to regain its grip on the land until she could no longer ignore the penetrating wind. Turning from the sandy hillock, she summoned the dog to follow. "Let's go, Bess."

With unusual disobedience, the dog stood still, ears alert, staring at the ice-covered lake.

"Come on, girl," Skye called. But again she ignored her mistress, and moved forward, whining deep in her throat.

Skye stopped and frowned huddling lower in her jacket. "What is it, girl?" The Newfoundland turned and whined again. "Okay, Bess—go."

The dog needed no further bidding. Barking sharply, she darted to the edge of the lake and scrambled awkwardly over the ice. Stopping suddenly, she stared down into a crack where several thick, rotting sheets had rammed together. Whining loudly, she pawed anxiously at the edge of the ice.

Hoping her trust in the dog's instincts justified the risky climb, Skye followed. "What is it, Bess? If this is just a game of yours—" Skye stopped and raised her head as her ears caught a faint wail.

"Oh, my God," she gasped. Her chest tightened as she leaned over the edge of the ice bank and saw the bright red of a child's jacket.

Within seconds, Skye had slid down the thick ice slab and was kneeling beside the trembling child. The crying stopped briefly as frightened blue eyes stared up at her and then started again in loud choking sobs.

"It's okay, sweetheart," Skye whispered, stroking a cold white cheek. "I'll get you out."

Conscious of the thrusting power of the wind against the unstable ice, Skye moved as quickly as possible within the narrow confines of the icy trap. Holding the child in her arms, she looked up to the whining dog, then with a quick boost, she raised the girl to the animal's level.

"Get her, Bess," she commanded. As the dog edged forward, the girl, obviously scared, began to struggle.

"She won't hurt you," Skye soothed, knowing how frightening the big Newfoundland could appear. "Bess is my friend—she'll help pull you out. Just put your arms around her neck—that's right!"

Small red-clad arms timidly clasped the dog's shaggy neck. Her teary blue eyes sought Skye's for approval.

"It's okay—you're almost out," Skye reassured with a warm smile. "Hang on tight. Bess is strong, but you'll have to help her by not letting go. Good! Now, back, Bess! Good dog!"

Within minutes the rescue was over. Alarmed by the child's pallor and the shudders that racked her fragile body, Skye scooped her up and walked rapidly, hurrying over the shore's rise, through clumps of barren willow, to a small green clapboard cottage.

As soon as they were inside, Skye set the girl on the couch then turned the baseboard heaters on high. She shrugged off her jacket and turned to the child. She tried to comfort her, offering the girl reassuring words as she removed her small sodden jacket and boots. "You'll be okay, sweetheart. My name is Skye," she told her. "What's yours?"

"Karin," she said hesitantly, hardly a thread of sound in her voice.

"Well, Karin," Skye smiled, stroking a halo of chestnut curls, "we're going to have to take off all these wet clothes. Will you let me help?"

Karin's response was a barely perceptible nod.

Working quickly, Skye removed the soaked sweater, jeans and tights. After briskly toweling the child's thin, shivering body, she pulled one of her sweatshirts over the little girl's head.

"There," Skye said as she rolled up the sleeves. "Is that better?" Again, she nodded slightly. "Good. Now I'm going to bundle you up in this blanket and then make you some cocoa. You'll soon be as warm as toast."

It took some time before Skye was satisfied that Karin was out of danger. The girl had finished a cup of cocoa and was lying on the couch wrapped snugly in a hunter-green woolly blanket, a warm pink flush replacing her icy pallor. Her clear blue eyes had lost their look of terror and were blinking drowsily. It was time to ask some questions, Skye thought. She had to locate the child's parents. They must be frantic by now!

"Karin," she began, gently rubbing the soft skin of the girl's wrist with her thumb, "we have to get you home. Do you live close by?"

"Don' know." The words were a sleepy murmur.

"Please, Karin," Skye said with a smile. "Try to stay awake for just a bit longer. You have to tell me where I can find your mother and father. They must be very worried about you."

Karin stiffened and shook her head, speaking with unexpected vigor. "I don't want to go back!" Tears welled in her eyes as she stared at Skye then started to cry.

Skye pulled her close, murmuring soothing words as she patted the small, shuddering back. She was surprised by the tears. Why didn't she want to go home? Most children would be crying to see their parents, not at the thought of returning to them. What was wrong?

Exhausted by her ordeal, Karin was soon asleep, a tiny frown marring her smooth forehead. Skye felt a rush of protectiveness as she gently wiped tears from the girl's flushed face.

She's so young, Skye thought. No more than five or six. She shouldn't have been anywhere near that lake by herself. And why was she so upset at the thought of going home?

Skye tucked the blanket closer around the sleeping child and sat thoughtfully, rubbing her thumb across her bottom lip. The only thing she could do was phone the police and let them know she had found the girl. Surely someone had been in touch with them. She stood up and reached for her jacket. The cottage had no phone, but there was a public one near the turnoff from the highway. She had no choice but to leave the child alone for a short while, but her trusted friend Bess was a good watchdog.

"Stay with her, Bess," she quietly commanded. "Good parents or bad, they have to know where she is."

It was almost dark and a scud of sullen cloud spat an icy rain, picked up and driven by the wind with stinging force. Skye jogged down the road, anxious to make the call and return before Karin woke up to find herself alone.

Almost half an hour had passed before Skye was back in the warmth of the tiny cottage. The dog looked up from the couch, where she had squeezed alongside Karin, and wagged her tail in welcome.

Karin was sleeping soundly. One thin arm had slipped out from the cocoon of blanket and was draped over the dog's neck. Skye leaned down and stroked a soft cheek gently, encouraged by its warmth.

She'll be all right, Skye thought. But why doesn't she want to go home? Was she simply overreacting to punishment for some childish misdemeanor, or did it go deeper than that? She sat on a kitchen chair facing the couch, puzzled.

The police had obviously been informed that Karin was missing, but oddly, hadn't given Skye any details. After she had given them the information they had told her that someone would be sent out immediately. That had been all. There was nothing she could do now but wait.

She certainly is a pretty little thing, Skye mused, her face softening with a smile. Her fingers instinctively reached for the pencil and sketch pad on the table beside her. With quick, sure strokes she drew the childish curve of cheek, the fan of dark gold lashes and the mop of unruly curls. Working rapidly, she added an outline of the dog with the child's arm curling around the thick, black neck.

There was still a baby softness about Karin in spite of her thinness, and it tugged at Skye's heart as her pencil moved over the paper. She isn't much older than Jennifer would have been, she thought and blinked back tears. Her hand slowed to a stop. Her eyes closed. *Jennifer*...

Skye was lost in her memories until a single, sharp rap on the door startled her. Before she knew what was happening it flew open with stunning suddenness and then slammed shut behind the man filling the entrance. His eyes, shadowed by the hood of a rain cape, swept over Skye to Karin.

"What happened?" His voice was harsh.

Skye moved quickly to stand beside the couch, her hand dropping to still the dog who bared her teeth in a warning growl. Skye, her heart still thudding from her alarm at his sudden entry, stared at the tall figure, but there was little to see but the hard, shadowed lines on his face. "Who are you?" she demanded, ignoring his question.

The man moved impatiently, shrugging off the concealing hood. "Her father," he said flatly.

Skye stared at him, knowing instantly he spoke the truth. His narrowed eyes were the same vivid blue as Karin's and just as thickly lashed. His curly hair was just a slightly deeper shade of chestnut. But his face had none of her soft smoothness. Deep lines etched his cheeks and framed his eyes, giving him a hard, uncompromising look.

Skye bit her lips, looking with apprehension from the man to the sleeping child. Even Bess was watching him warily, every protective instinct aroused, still growling deep in her throat.

"Call off that damned dog," he demanded testily.

"That 'damned dog' saved your daughter's life today, and she thinks you're going to hurt the child," Skye said coldly, moving closer to the side of the couch, her face clearly showing that she felt the same way.

"Hurt her!" The man looked at Skye, a brief flash of astonishment softening his features, then his face hardened again and he glared angrily. "Is that what you think? That's the last thing I'd do!"

"Is it?" Skye folded her arms across her chest and stared unwaveringly at him. "That's one terrified little girl, mister, and it wasn't just what happened this afternoon that scared her, either."

To her surprise, his broad shoulders slumped with a weary sigh and his hands moved displaying a helpless gesture. "What did happen?" he asked, his voice quieter.

Skye studied him warily, not trusting this sudden mood change. But he didn't look at her. Rather he stared at his daughter with an unguarded expression of bewildered longing, which puzzled Skye. His look was one that somehow indicated to Skye that this man, however rude, did care about the girl. So Skye related what had happened by the lake.

"I think she's okay now," she finished. "She was mainly cold and wet—she seems to have warmed up."

He crouched and held out a hand to Bess. "Good dog," he said in a low voice. Bess moved her tail in acquiescence and licked the big hand.

Skye relaxed perceptibly. She trusted the dog's instincts absolutely, knowing Bess would quickly sense any hidden anger or aggression. No, this man would not harm them.

She watched as he urged Bess from the couch and sat down beside his daughter. His hand moved with tenderness over the tangled curls and soft brow, his fingers curling as he stroked the curve of her cheek. He turned to look up at Skye. "Thank you." The words were quietly sincere.

With a half smile, Skye nodded, oddly comforted by his gratitude. But as he began to gather Karin into his arms, she became alarmed, "What are you doing?"

"Taking her home," he said, tucking the blanket tightly around his daughter. "I'll return your things tomorrow."

"But—you can't go," Skye protested. "It's cold and raining."

"Karin should be at home," he said, standing up with her in his arms, "and I think a doctor ought to take a look at her."

Skye nodded in understanding but still felt anxious for Karin. She had been so upset at the thought of going home, and Skye still didn't know why. Was she being mistreated? If not by this man, perhaps someone else?

"What was she doing down by the lake by herself like that?" Her question was blunt and unexpected, her direct look demanding an answer.

He dropped his hand from the doorknob. "She must have wandered down there instead of coming directly home from where the school bus lets her off," he said briefly. "I appreciate your concern, but I assure you Karin is well taken care of." A smile fleetingly touched his lips. "Thank you—both." With that, he went out the door, closing it quietly behind him.

Skye stared at the door. Of course he had to go, she reasoned, stroking the dog's head. A doctor should examine her, and her mother must be beside herself with worry. But over all her reasoning, Skye could still see a vivid picture of the anguish in Karin's blue eyes, and her heart was touched with pity and concern.

She thought of the tall, attractive man and the way his strong hand moved with such obvious tenderness over his daughter's curls. "She'll be all right," she murmured to Bess in an effort to convince herself. "Anyway, there isn't anything we can do about it."

Her father would be back the next day to return her shirt and blanket. Maybe she could arrange to see Karin again, to reassure herself about the child's safety.

Her concern was more than just a natural reaction to what had happened this afternoon. The baby softness still evident in the little girl had struck a chord of memory. With a faraway look in her eyes, Skye went over to a cupboard and pulled out a suitcase. She opened it, and removed the folded clothes that sheltered a small painting. She sat on the edge of the bed and stared at it.

It was a portrait of a baby done in soft watercolors and enclosed by a simple silver frame. As always, the infant's laughing silver-gray eyes brought a smile to Skye's lips, desperate longing to smooth the fine, dusky curls, but there was nothing to touch save the coldness of the protective glass. Sweet, sweet Jennifer. With a last, lingering look, she tucked away the painting and sighed shakily.

Abruptly, Skye stood up and crossed the floor to her easel. She hastily squeezed a tube of crimson acrylic paint onto the palette and jabbed a brush into it. She took a deep, steadying breath and carefully stroked the brush onto the canvas. Then, as had happened so many times, she lost herself in the magic of creating.

The hours passed unnoticed. Skye had been aware only of the work in front of her until the dog, with an almost apologetic look, whined at the door to be let out. She put down the brush, suddenly conscious of a deep inner weariness.

"Hang on, Bess, old girl. I'll come with you." A brisk walk would relax her muscles, which were tense from long hours of concentration.

A short walk brought them to the lake. The wind had died down and most of the clouds were gone. The darkness was softened by starlight reflecting on the white sand and the lake was calm except for a hollow lapping of waves under the ice. Skye walked rapidly, the big dog never far from her side. As soon as she felt tired enough to ensure an easy sleep, she turned and jogged back to the cottage. But sleep didn't come easily for Skye. Her mind was taken up with thoughts of the day's events. She could still see the frightened look in Karin's eyes—and the strong and puzzling man who had carried her away.

MORNING STARTED with Bess's sharp warning bark followed by a loud knocking on the door. Yawning, Skye threw back the blankets and slid out of bed. She pulled on the fleecy bottoms of a sweat suit and looked unsuccessfully for the top. As the knocking started again, she reached for the old flannel shirt that she used as a painting smock and buttoned it quickly. "Okay, I'm coming," she murmured.

She whipped open the door and stared into a pair of vivid sky-blue eyes. Their somewhat derisive expression and the quirk in one shaggy eyebrow made her aware of how disheveled she must look.

"I woke you up," he stated.

Skye pushed her tight, tangled curls back from her face and blinked sleepily. "That's all right, I'm sure it's time I was up, anyway. How's Karin—is she okay?"

"She's fine, thanks to you." In spite of the warmth of his words, the strong face remained impassive.

Does he ever smile? Skye wondered. Stepping back, she opened the door wider. "Come in," she invited.

"Thank you, but I have to get back. I just came to return your blanket and shirt." He handed her a freshly washed and neatly folded bundle.

Skye flashed a quick smile. "Thank you. Just a minute," she added as he turned to leave. "Karin's clothes are still here—I'll get them." As she returned with the clothes, she noticed her sketch of Karin and the dog and impulsively, she tore it from the pad.

"Here you go," she said, handing the clothes and boots to him. "And..." she hesitated, "maybe Karin would like this." She gave him the drawing.

He looked at it and then at her in surprise. "This is very good," he said.

"Thank you," Skye said, feeling her cheeks grow warm. His direct, appraising look made her feel as though he was seeing her for the first time. "You don't mind if she keeps it?"

"Not at all," he said. "I'm sure she'll be delighted," he added turning to go.

"Wait," Skye called impulsively , slightly surprised by her forwardness. He turned back to her, one eyebrow raised in query. "I just wanted to know," she added "do you live nearby?"

"About half a mile north along the lake," he answered.

"Good. I mean—maybe I'll get a chance to see Karin again." Her tone was questioning.

He stood just a short distance from the open door, his eyes fastening on hers for a moment, their blue depths expressionless. "Maybe," he said briefly, his lips moving in a semblance of a smile. "Goodbye."

Before she could say anything, he had disappeared through the willows lining the sandy lakeshore. Skye shrugged and went back inside, thinking ruefully that he hadn't seemed very enthusiastic about her seeing Karin again.

And no wonder! she suddenly thought with a grimace, looking around at the single-room cottage cluttered to no end with paints and brushes and all sorts of art supplies. He must think I'm somewhat disreputable. She made another wry face as she looked at her reflection in the spotted mirror hanging over the big porcelain kitchen sink. "Make that thoroughly disreputable!" she muttered to her reflection.

Her tight, dark curls, with their usual disregard for order, looked as though they hadn't seen a brush in days, and shadows underlined her silver-gray eyes. She glanced down at her bare feet, at the faded, baggy sweat pants and at the paint-spattered flannel shirt and grinned. There was no doubt she must have looked a touch unsavory, certainly not the type of woman parents would want their young children to spend time with.

She decided it was time to shape up, as she turned away from the mirror. This general disregard for her appearance had begun when she'd left Reid—and the closets of clothing he had carefully selected for her.

Sure, she was always clean and fairly neat, but she hadn't realized just how scruffy she had begun to look.

She ran her fingers through her hair, remembering how Reid had disliked the unruly curls. He would have preferred her hair to be as smooth and sleek and dull as the clothes he bought for her, but he had settled for a close cut that gave it some kind of order. She hadn't had it cut in the two years since she had left him—just another form of rebellion against the controls he had imposed on her during their marriage. How many times, since she'd been on her own, had she done something simply because she knew he would have disapproved? And the incongruity of the situation was that Reid did not and would not ever know.

She slowly unbuttoned her shirt and slid out of the sweat pants, reaching for a towel as she went to the tiny shower cubicle in the corner of the room. He's been dead for almost two years, she told herself grimly as she stepped under the hot spray. Wasn't it time she stopped rebelling?

SKYE HADN'T REALIZED what a nuisance being without transportation would be. She was beginning to wish she'd rented a car when she took her van into the garage in town for an extensive overhaul, but at the time she'd thought she could manage easily enough without one.

She should have stocked up on groceries, she thought, eyeing the few remaining contents in the fridge. She'd had her fill of vegetable soup and peanut butter sandwiches.

She glanced at the clock on the wall above the stove. It was still early and there was plenty of time for her to take a walk to the gas station down the highway. The small convenience shop there had a limited selection of groceries for local trade. Maybe she could find something interesting to cook up for tonight's meal.

"You stay home, Bess," she said as she rolled up a knapsack and stuffed it into her shoulder bag. The dog immediately slumped down on the floor and watched dejectedly as Skye pulled on a jacket and left.

It was a lovely day. The cold winds and rain of the days before had vanished and the air was once again soft and warm. The sun, growing in strength each day, penetrated deep into the soil, releasing a rich, earthy odor that promised new growth. The willow bushes and balsam poplar that lined the gravel drive leading to the highway seemed about to burst into life and added the sweet smell of rising sap into the air.

Skye breathed deeply and paused to look around, glad she had made the last-minute decision to take the cottage on the shore of Lake Winnipeg rather than return to Vancouver as she had originally planned. She had met the owners in Texas during her winter travels and they had offered her the use of their cottage for all of May and most of June. The ice had completely covered the lake when she'd arrived, although the snow was gone from the land. Day by day, it had been a thrill to watch the frozen chunks break up.

Squinting, she looked up at the sky that dominated the scene. With the far, flat horizons of the prairie there was nothing to stunt its magnificence and it demanded to be watched as clouds and light played across its vast, blue surface. A flock of snow geese, sun flashing on their wings, flew low and noisily toward the lake. Skye smiled happily and started walking again, a slight spring in her step.

The highway, serving the small towns and farms along the lake, eventually led into Winnipeg. But this far from the city, there was rarely any traffic, and Skye walked along at a comfortable pace, trying to remember if there was a coffee shop at the gas station. She suddenly had a craving for a cheeseburger, with loads of onions and relish.

Skye heard a car coming up behind her, and to her surprise, the driver slowed as he passed and then pulled to a stop on the opposite shoulder. Skye kept walking, keeping a wary eye on the car as she came closer. As she reached the car, she saw the driver's window being rolled down.

"I thought it was you," a deep voice called, and even from across the highway she recognized those striking blue eyes. "Would you like a ride?"

"Yes, I would." Skye crossed the road and slipped quickly inside, shutting the door. "Thank you."

"No problem," he said. "How far are you going?"

"Just to the gas station," Skye answered casually. "I need a few groceries."

He glanced at her. "Well, you won't get a lot there—they don't carry much more than milk and bread and maybe a few canned goods."

"I know—but I'd settle for a bag of potato chips at this point. I'm getting very low on things."

"Don't you have a car?"

"A van—it's in Gimli being repaired. I thought it would be ready by now, but the poor old thing needed a lot of work and parts had to be ordered in, so..." She shrugged. "I haven't really missed it, but I'm getting awfully tired of soup and peanut butter sandwiches."

He hesitated briefly, sparing a few seconds from the road to look at her. "I'm going in to Gimli," he said finally. "If you like, I can drop you off at a grocery store and pick you up again after I run a couple of errands."

"Oh, I don't want to be any bother," Skye said politely.

"It's no bother. I expect to be about an hour—will that be enough time for you?"

"More than enough, thank you." She was silent for a few moments, watching the endless stretches of farmland along the highway. "How is Karin?" she asked, turning to look at him.

She noticed a bleak, shadowed look flicker across his face. "She's fine," he answered. "She's back in school today." His voice was even toned and impersonal, and his eyes remained fixed on the road.

"I'm glad she's all right," Skye tired to show some enthusiasm. "What grade is she in?"

"Kindergarten. She goes in the afternoons."

"So she's what—five?"

"Yes," he said listlessly.

Skye stiffled a sigh. From his brief, almost curt answers she had to assume that he didn't want to talk. She felt bad for she would have loved to hear more about how Karin was doing. Even just chatting about the district would be enough. Too many days went by without any human contact, and Skye missed the companionship.

As the miles slipped by, she grew more and more curious about the man beside her. Her silver-gray eyes stole quick, sidelong glances at him, but his eyes remained on the road, his face a picture of cold remoteness.

He'd be very handsome, Skye thought, if he wasn't so...so dour looking. The lines on his face were even more pronounced in the sunlit interior of the car and his taut mouth hadn't relaxed at all. His eyes seemed a contradiction to the rest of his face. The contrast of blue with his thick, dark-gold lashes was startling. Most women would kill for eyes like that, Skye thought with a trace of a smile.

I wonder what he does for a living, she mused. Farm, perhaps, or fish? The long, square-tipped fingers gripping the steering wheel showed no obvious signs of manual labor. Then it dawned on her that she didn't even know the man's name! Skye shifted her position slightly so as to face him. Well, she told herself, she wouldn't find out anything unless she asked. "You know," she said, looking at him directly, "I don't even know your name. I guess we never did get a chance for introductions."

He paused then turned to look at her. "Bjorn Stefansson," he said finally. "What's yours?"

"Skye Cameron. You're of Icelandic descent?" she queried, wanting to keep up some kind of conversation.

"Like most of the people in the district," he answered with a trace of amusement in his voice. "And Cameron—that's what? Scottish? Or is it your husband's name?"

Surprised by his inquiry, Skye flexed her left hand and stared at the thick gold band on her finger. "I kept my maiden name," she said and added, after a brief hesitation, "I—I'm a widow." Technically it was true, but the words felt like a lie. She looked out the window.

"I'm sorry." There was an unexpected gentleness in the deep voice. "Has it been long?"

"About a year and a half." Her brief reply clearly stated that she didn't want to talk about it. She felt guilty when people offered her sympathy, but the truth was too complicated. She had left Reid, but he had died before she could divorce him. The ring was not Reid's; it was her mother's. Far from ready to become involved with another man, Skye had started wearing it to discourage men from asking her out. The words, "I'm a widow," from one so young seemed to take men aback and rarely did anyone bother to persist.

Again there was silence between them but this time it was a tension-filled silence. Well, Skye concluded, they had nothing to talk about—just idle small talk. They were strangers who had shared a momentary bond over a little girl. If they weren't living fairly close along a relatively isolated section of the lake, she probably would never have seen him again. Skye felt relieved when they finally entered the town.

Bjorn pulled up beside a supermarket. "I'll meet you here in about an hour," he told her as she opened the car door. "And, uh—Skye—I'm sorry if I upset you back there."

Skye looked at him, holding his eyes for a moment, surprised at his concern, "It's okay," she smiled briefly. "See you in an hour." She got out quickly and shut the door.

She watched him drive away. Giving her head a little shake, she turned to go into the store and then changed her mind. Deciding to make the best use of the little time she had, she hurried up the main street.

First she checked on the van and was told they were still waiting for a part, which would probably arrive later that week. After that, she went to the bank to transfer some money from her Vancouver account and then rushed back to the grocery store. Anxious not to keep Bjorn waiting, she quickly picked up the items she needed and hurried through the checkout. He was waiting when she came out.

"Is that all you're getting?" he asked as she stowed the single bag on the back seat and slid in beside him. "You should have stocked up."

"There's enough," she assured him. "I don't eat much."

His shoulders moved in a shrug as he eased the car through the sparse traffic back to the highway. Skye settled back prepared for the silence of the return drive—and silent it was until they were turning onto the narrow gravel drive leading to the cottage. "Are you renting from the Siguardsons?" Bjorn asked, then pulled to a stop near the door.

"Borrowing, actually," Skye said as she opened the car door and pulled the seat forward to retrieve her groceries. "I met them traveling in the States this winter and they offered it to me for a couple of months." She smiled. "It isn't much, but after living in the van for so long, it feels great."

"You live in your van?" He was frowning slightly and seemed almost shocked. "Don't you have a home somewhere?"

"No." The word was terse. A home was something she'd had for too brief a time in childhood. She glanced up and found him observing her, a perplexed look in his eyes. And why wouldn't he be puzzled, she thought. How could anyone with a home and family understand why she kept moving? Clutching the bag of groceries to her chest, she got out of the car.

"Thank you, Mr. Stefansson," she intoned politely. "I appreciate the ride."

"Wait—Skye." He hesitated as she leaned into the car to look at him. "Would you like to come over for dinner tonight? I know Mary is cooking a roast. There'll be plenty."

"That's very kind of you, Mr. Stefansson," Skye said politely, "but I don't think it would be fair to intrude on your wife's meal plans unannounced."

"My wife!" The startled blue eyes held hers for a moment before he spoke again. "Mary is my house-keeper."

"But—Karin's mother..."

"Karin's mother is dead."

The words were harsh and flat, but Skye scarcely noticed in the rush of renewed sympathy for the child. "Oh, the poor baby!" she exclaimed. "Has it been long?"

"Three months."

Three months! No wonder he looked so grim, so preoccupied—and Karin...Skye's heart went out to that frightened and hurt little girl. She sat down on the edge of the car seat. "I'm sorry," she murmured with heart-felt sympathy.

"Forget it." His voice was brusque. "About dinner—"

"I really don't want to intrude."

Just then, to her surprise, he leaned across the seat and touched her hand. "You're most welcome in my home," he said softly. "You saved my daughter's life."

Skye looked at him and their eyes locked for a long moment. The unexpected intimacy of his gaze almost frightened her. Unlike the set lines of his face, the eyes showed emotion and she caught his vulnerability in their depths.

"Please come." She felt his fingers tighten briefly on hers and there was just a hint of a plea in his voice. "I think Karin would like to see you again." The thought of seeing the child again made up Skye's mind.

"All right." she agreed. "When?"

"Now, if you want. I'll wait."

Skye shook her head. "Thanks, but I think I'll walk over later. I have some things to do. Is it all right if I bring Bess?"

"The dog? Of course." He released her hand and straightened up in his seat. "It's the first house north of here—about half a mile if you follow the lake. Come anytime before six."

Skye nodded and got out of the car. "I'll see you later, then." She closed the door, watching the dusty gravel spray up behind his car, still feeling the imprint of his fingers on her warm hand. She was puzzled. Why had his mood changed so abruptly? One minute he had been cool and distant as if he didn't care to acknowledge her presence. The next he had practically pleaded with her to come for dinner. Perhaps his distance, his aloofness, hadn't been against her personally, but was somehow connected to his grief over the loss of his wife. Three months was too short a time for him to have come to terms with her death. And Karin—how hard it must be for her. But that still didn't explain his mood changes, Skye thought as she went into the cottage.

The dog greeted her enthusiastically and then scampered outside for a run. Skye put the groceries away and then sat down, drumming her fingers restlessly on the tabletop.

She usually accepted social invitations. Her solitary travels would be too lonely otherwise. But this invitation was different. Tonight there wouldn't be the usual exchange of experiences and humorous stories shared with fellow travelers. She had clearly seen the little girl's distress and had sensed the man's. Biting her lip, she stood up. Her own sorrows were dangerously close to the surface. Could she risk becoming involved in theirs?

As she opened the door for the dog, she had a clear picture of Karin's tear-filled eyes, her trembling lips and knew she wanted to see the child again. Bending down on level with the dog's massive head, she fondled her silky black ears. "Hey, Bess, old girl, want to go out for dinner tonight?"

CHAPTER TWO

SKYE HAD NO TROUBLE finding the house. Tall trees kept it well hidden from the lake, but a broad path lead from one corner of the yard to the sandy shore. It was an old Manitoba farmhouse, which had undergone extensive renovations. The original two-story section of cream-colored stone melded perfectly with a modern addition of golden cedar. High windows in a cathedral slope looked through the trees to the lake, and a multilevel deck extended along the back wall.

She walked toward the house admiring the scene. The yards were extensive, the grass tinged with a healthy springtime green and was dotted, parklike, with elm and oak trees yet to foliate. She imagined how beautiful it would be in summer, when all the shrubs and trees were in leaf. Followed closely by Bess, she crossed the lawn to a side door off the deck and knocked.

The door opened immediately. "You must be Skye—come in!" The words of welcome were issued by a tiny, gray-haired woman with a plump, smiling face and warm hazel eyes.

"I'm Mary Sawchuck." She beamed, standing aside to let Skye in. "No, no—bring the dog in," she insisted as Skye ordered Bess to wait outside. "You're both very welcome."

"Thank you," Skye said and stepped into the kitchen. "I hope my being here is no bother."

"Of course it isn't—there's always plenty of food. Here, let me take your jacket. Bjorn is upstairs with Karin. They'll be down in a minute. In the meantime, I'm supposed to take you into the living room and offer you a drink."

"Would it be all right if I stayed here with you?" Skye asked. "It's such a lovely room."

"It is, isn't it?" Mary agreed. "Why don't you sit there." She pointed to a breakfast counter near a large picture window.

Signaling for Bess to lie near the door, Skye pulled out a stool and sat down. The kitchen was in the older section of the house but had been completely renovated. It was bright and modern with overtones of country charm.

"Bjorn tells me you're staying at the Siguardsons'," Mary said as she bustled around the kitchen.

Skye nodded. "Yes—I met them in Texas in February. When they found out I'd never spent any time in Manitoba, they offered to let me use their cottage for a couple of months. I'm glad I decided to come. I like it here."

Mary stopped her bustle and sighed. "You women today—you're so lucky. In my day we married and stayed with our husbands—or didn't marry and stayed with our parents. You're lucky to have so many choices." Suddenly she put her hand to her mouth, her eyes widening with distress. "Oh, I'm sorry! Bjorn told me about your loss. How thoughtless of me!"

That horrible lie again, Skye thought grimly, wishing it wasn't so awkward to explain. She hastened to reassure Mary. "It's okay—really. Don't worry about it." She smiled brightly and changed the subject. "Dinner smells wonderful."

"I hope you're hungry," Mary said, with a quick, still-apologetic look. She opened the oven door and lifted out the roast.

"Starving," Skye admitted, her mouth watering under a barrage of delicious aromas. "I haven't eaten since this morning and then it was just toast."

Mary shook her head and clucked disapprovingly. "No wonder you're so thin. You should eat more," she said, putting the pan on the counter.

"I know," Skye admitted. "I just forget sometimes."

"Artists!" Mary shook her head again, then added, "Karin showed me the drawing of her and the dog. You know, you're really very good." Mary began stirring some sort of sauce.

"Thank you. I hope she liked it."

"Loved it. It's hardly been out of her sight since Bjorn gave it to her. You know," Mary paused and looked thoughtful, "you made quite an impression on that girl."

"I did?" Skye was surprised. "I didn't think she would really remember me. She was asleep most of the time."

"Well, she's talked about you and the dog ever since. Not," Mary added, "that she talks much. She's a quiet child—too quiet."

"She must miss her mother," Skye said softly.

Mary raised her eyebrows in surprise. "Bjorn told you about Debbie, his late wife?"

"Only that she had died recently. Mary," Skye wanted to change the subject, "is there anything I can do to help you?"

"Not a thing. Everything is under control—just sit right there and keep me company."

Skye obeyed, watching as Mary drained and seasoned the vegetables. Where were Karin and Bjorn? She was only half looking forward to the evening ahead. She did want to see Karin again and the meal promised to be excellent, but what about Bjorn? Would he be as dour and uncommunicative as he had been on their drive into Gimli?

Just then Bjorn entered the kitchen, pushing through the louvered doors, Karin trailing behind him. "So—you did come." There was a mild welcome in his deep voice, but no change in his expression. "Karin—say hello to Ms Cameron."

"Oh, please call me Skye," she said hastily. "Hello, Karin. How are you?"

Karin looked at the floor. "Fine," she whispered shyly.

"My dog, Bess, came with me," Skye went on, touched by the child's timidity. "Would you like to say hello to her?"

The chestnut curls bobbed ever so slightly.

"She's over by the door," Skye said. "She'll be happy to see you."

Looking up cautiously, the child stood still for a moment longer, then moved slowly to the door. She stole a quick, sidelong look at Skye, her blue eyes appearing huge in her thin face.

Skye glanced at Bjorn and Mary. Both were watching the girl with identical looks of concern, and she herself was touched by Karin's shy hesitancy. She rose from the stool and crossed the floor to where Karin stood with uncertainty by the dog.

"Bess is happy to see you again, Karin. Aren't you, girl?" Hearing her name, the dog swept her feathery tail across the floor. Skye knelt down and smiled at Karin, holding out a hand to her. "She loves little girls."

Karin hesitated and then slowly put her cold small hand into Skye's. "She's big."

Skye nodded. "Yes, she is—but very gentle. Remember the picture I drew? Well, that's exactly what happened while you were sleeping. She couldn't wait to sneak up onto the couch and cuddle with you." Skye rubbed the dog's ears affectionately. "She's just a great big teddy bear."

Dropping Skye's hand, Karin reached out to the dog tentatively. Bess's tail wagged harder and her large pink tongue swiped at the small hand. Then, so soft and short it was almost missed, a giggle bubbled from the girl's lips. "It tickles," she whispered and smiled shyly at Skye.

Skye smiled back, resisting an urge to hug her. "It does, doesn't it?" she agreed and stood up to make more room for Karin beside the dog. Instantly the girl crouched down, patting the massive head. "Nice doggie," she said, her voice stronger.

Skye turned to find both Bjorn and Mary looking at her. Mary was smiling slightly and nodding her head as though she had reached a kind of silent conclusion. Bjorn's expression was inscrutable.

"Bjorn," Mary said brightly, "why don't you fix Skye that drink she wouldn't take from me. Supper will be about ten minutes yet." She turned back to the stove.

Bjorn was watching Skye, his eyes reflective. "Come on," he said, inclining his head toward the doorway.

Skye smiled warily and followed him. For some reason, this man made her feel nervous. Usually she could talk to strangers with ease, but his reticence left her tongue-tied. They went down a short hallway leading to the newer part of the house. Stopping at the top of a short flight of stairs, Skye stood staring. "Fantastic," she said finally.

The huge room had a high, sloping ceiling crossed with wooden beams. The room was divided by the placement of furniture and large, leafy plants into a living area, a dining area, and with the addition of an antique rolltop desk, a work area. An overstuffed couch and matching chairs sat in front of a massive stone fireplace. On each side of the hearth were long, wide windows, with cushions piled invitingly underneath where one could watch the fire or cast their eyes on the breathtaking view of the yard and the lake beyond.

Skye loved it. She turned to the man beside her. "Bjorn—it's perfect!" Her usual enthusiasm was back. "You're lucky to live here."

Bjorn's expression was difficult to read, but he seemed pleased. "It is something, isn't it? My sister Lara designed it."

"She's very talented."

He nodded in agreement. "Very. She's a successful architect in Toronto, specializing in remodeling older homes. She also doubles in interior design. She did this as a favor for me when I decided to move back."

"You haven't always lived here?" Skye crossed the room to look out the big windows.

"No, my mother, sister and I moved East after my father died. This was my grandparents' place. I bought if from them when they sold the farm."

"Are they still living?" Skye asked, running her fingers over the rough stone of the fireplace.

He shook his head. "They died before I was able to move back. The place was empty for several years."

"Funny, it feels as though it has always been lived in." Her voice was soft. Then Skye noticed that embedded in the cream-colored stone was an ancient snail shell. "There's a fossil!" she exclaimed, her tone upbeat again.

Bjorn walked toward her. "This is Tyndal stone," he explained, standing close beside her. "It's quarried near Tyndal—a small town south of here." Skye couldn't help but notice the firm lines of his jaw, his vivid blue eyes, as he spoke. "All the rock is full of marine fossils, remnants of the inland sea that once covered most of the prairies." Bjorn observed her thin, sensitive fingers stroke the stone as her mysterious, silver-gray eyes absorbed the details of the unusual rock. Suddenly she turned her head and looked up at him with a smile.

"What do you do?" she asked disarmingly, hoping she wasn't prying. "For a living, I mean?"

Bjorn ran his fingers through his chestnut curls. "I write," he told her simply.

Sensing that Skye was interested, he added, "Adventure stories for children, based on some of the old Icelandic sagas." His lips twitched as though he might smile.

"That sounds very interesting," Skye said. She sat down and leaned against the hearth. "Are you able to read Icelandic?"

He lowered himself to sit on the hearth. "Some," he answered, "but I rely on more scholarly translations for my information."

"I'd like to read them sometime," Skye said, hugging her knees to her chest.

"They're children's stories," he warned. "You probably wouldn't find them all that interesting."

"I'm sure I would," she said seriously. Skye had a love for all books. She looked up as Mary arrived with a tray in her hands. "Oh good—supper's ready. I'm starving," Skye confessed with childlike enthusiasm, and with a grin jumped to her feet.

Bjorn got up more slowly. "I thought you looked like you could use a good meal. Especially when I saw the size of that bag of groceries you took home today."

"Is that why you asked me over—to fatten me up?" Her eyes sparkled with a playful smile.

Again his lips twitched. "Of course," he said. "And..."

"And?" she prompted, eyeing him curiously.

He hesitated, watching his daughter enter the room with slow steps and downcast eyes. His expression brooding as he turned back to Skye. "I'd like to talk to you after supper."

Skye had watched him as he observed his daughter with concern. "About Karin?" she asked intuitively, her voice low.

He ran a hand through his hair and frowned deeply. "Yes. I— Well, it'll wait."

Skye was puzzled and slightly anxious as to what he could possibly want to talk to her about, but she found dinner was relaxed surprisingly, anyway. The food was delicious and Mary's bright chatter made up for Bjorn's lack of words and Karin's silence. Mary encouraged Skye to talk about her travels and she found herself chatting freely about the past winter, which she'd spent in the southern United States along the Gulf of Mexico from Florida to Texas, and how she would paint pictures of local scenes and sell them at roadside camps and shopping centers.

"Just you and the dog?" Bjorn questioned, looking at her thoughtfully.

"Just me and the dog," Skye echoed softly. Before anyone could comment, she changed the subject, asking Karin a question about her school.

Soon everyone pitched in to help Mary clear the table and load the dishwasher. Mary was more than a housekeeper to the Stefanssons. She was obviously very close to Karin and Bjorn, and her friendly, caring nature made for a comfortable, homey atmosphere. How different, Skye mused watching Bjorn carry a stack of dishes back to the kitchen, than the cold formality of Reid's house. She frowned and shook her head. She didn't want to think about Reid.

Bjorn lit a fire after the clean-up was finished and they all sat cozily around the hearth. Karin sat beside Skye, glancing at her shyly from time to time, but said nothing unless she was asked a direct question. Her answers were always short and spoken in a faint, whispery voice. Conversation still consisted mainly of Mary's chatter and various questions directed toward Skye. Bjorn listened with interest but, except for an occasional comment, was quiet.

Skye found herself watching Karin more and more. The child was far too quiet for her age and was obviously unhappy. Skye's heart contracted with pity.

When Mary mentioned bedtime, Karin stood up immediately with none of a child's usual protestations. She glanced at Skye from the corner of her eye and whispered something to Mary, who looked surprised. Turning to Skye, she said, "Karin would like you to come upstairs with us."

"I'd like that very much, Karin." Skye smiled at the child holding out her hand. Again there was a noticeable hesitation before Karin placed her hand in Skye's.

On the way out of the room, Skye paused in front of Bjorn, expecting Karin to kiss her father good-night. He reached out a hand to touch his daughter. Karin's movement wasn't quite a flinch, but she turned quickly away, avoiding her father's hand, hunching a shoulder to hide her averted face.

Skye watched Bjorn's hand clench helplessly and his face settle into bleaker lines. "Good night, Karin," he managed evenly. "Pleasant dreams." He turned away as they left the room.

The bedrooms were upstairs in the older section of the house. Skye and Karin followed Mary up the freshly polished oak staircase. Karin's room was brightly colored in yellows and greens and had shelves of books and toys. What a contrast to the rather austere dormitories of her own childhood, Skye thought.

Karin was still quiet. She snuck quick glances at Skye but remained silent as Mary bustled her through bedtime preparations.

"There you go, pet. All clean and ready for bed." Mary gave her a hug and kissed her cheek. "Hop in now."

But Karin didn't hop into bed. She sat on the edge and slowly eased under the covers. Instantly she closed herself into a tight little ball, hugging her knees against her thin chest. Skye could feel her own compassion reflected in Mary's concerned eyes as she tucked in the blankets.

"Mary," she asked impulsively, "could I stay with her for a minute?"

Mary smiled and nodded. "Of course," she said as she left the room. Somehow Skye couldn't bring herself to just leave the sad child alone. "Karin," Skye suggested gently, "would you like me to read a story to you?"

She nodded her small head slightly.

"Do you have a favorite book? Something special that you would like to hear?"

A thin shoulder shrugged.

Skye examined the shelves of books. There was no clue as to what might be a favorite. All of them had a shiny new look as though they had hardly been touched. She picked out *A Child's Garden of Verse* and settled herself on the edge of the bed.

"I'll read you a few of these poems. I liked them when I was a little girl." She dimmed the bedside lamp and leafed through the book, reading her favorite poems, her voice low and rhythmic.

When she finished and closed the book, Skye lightly touched the soft chestnut curls. "Good night, Karin," she said quietly. "Come and visit me soon, okay?" The child didn't answer. Skye turned out the light.

She paused in the doorway and looked back. Karin's eyes had been so sad and solemn and Skye's heart had gone out to her just a little bit more. No child should ever be that unhappy. Forcing a smile, she brought her fingers to her lips and blew a kiss across the room. "Sweet dreams, Karin," she whispered.

She went back downstairs frowning reflectively. She could hear Mary in the kitchen as she went through the hallway to the living room. Bjorn was standing with his back to her, staring into the fire.

Skye paused and stood watching him for a moment. What had caused the rift between him and his daugh-

ter—misunderstandings related to his wife's death?
Skye's lips moved wryly. She was quickly becoming
concerned about this family's problems. Perhaps too
concerned. The child had certainly touched her heart.
And who could be immune to the anguish that lurked
behind the father's brooding face? She hid a sigh as he
sensed her presence and turned toward her.

His look was long and pensive. He leaned against the
mantel with his hands in the pockets of his slacks, his
eyes hooded and intense as though he was judging her.

"I read her a story—well, poems, actually," Skye
found herself explaining, growing nervous under his
stare. "I—I hope I didn't impose."

He shook his head. "On the contrary. It was very
considerate of you. Please, have a seat," he invited.
"Mary is bringing in coffee. Would you like some
brandy?"

"Yes, thank you." Skye sat on the plump and comfortable couch facing the fire. She watched as he crossed
to a wall unit in the dining area and poured some
brandy from a decanter, examining his profile and the
deep line cutting his cheek. He still hasn't smiled, she
thought, not once—but he looks as though he was
meant to smile, as though those lines were laugh lines.
What would his smile be like, she wondered.

She continued to observe him as he strode back toward her, drinks in hand. His lean body moved easily,
with an appealing masculine grace. He had, she reflected with narrowed eyes, the type of presence she
would like to paint. She cocked her head and smiled as
he handed her a glass. "I was just thinking that you
would make a good subject to paint."

His thick eyebrows rose in surprise. "I would?"

"Definitely. I could put you in any kind of setting—you know, in a fishing boat fighting the elements, or at the prow of a Viking ship. Something like that."

His eyes lightened with amusement. "What about hunched over a typewriter? That's what I seem to do most of the time."

"That, too," Skye replied, leaning back against the cushions and sipping her brandy. "How long have you been writing?"

"Professionally, about three years." He dropped lithely onto a cushion beside the hearth.

"And before that?"

"I was just another cog in a big corporate wheel," he said dismissively, as though that kind of life was long behind him.

At that moment Mary came in with the coffee tray. Bjorn leaped up to take it from her and placed it on a small brass-trimmed glass table. "Thanks, Mary—join us for a drink?"

Mary sat down on the couch and stretched out her legs. "A small sherry please, Bjorn, and then I'm off to watch *Dynasty*. I never miss it," she confessed to Skye. "Although I hate to admit it." She took the sherry from Bjorn. "Thank you," she smiled.

He nodded and returned to his position beside the fire, staring silently into the flames as Mary talked to Skye about various TV programs. Skye sipped her drink and made appropriate comments, but her attention was drawn to the perturbingly enigmatic male on the floor across from her. He's unhappy, she realized—as unhappy as his daughter.

When she looked back at Mary she found the older woman studying her, a knowing look in her eyes. Oddly she nodded at Skye as though some how she knew her thoughts and was agreeing with her.

"I'm going to my room now, Skye," she said quietly. She inclined her head toward Bjorn. "Talk to him," she whispered. Ignoring Skye's startled look, she stood up. "Good night, Bjorn," she called.

He looked up, surprised. "Already? Well—good night, Mary. See you in the morning."

Skye watched her leave, feeling puzzled. Talk to him—about what? Karin? She had no idea what Mary meant.

They sat in silence for a few minutes. Bjorn wrapped long fingers around one knee and leaned back against the hearth. Nervous again, Skye waited for him to speak. He'd said earlier that he wanted to talk to her. His words were unexpected.

"Tell me honestly," he inquired suddenly, fixing unwavering eyes on her. "What do you think of Karin?"

Through her surprise, Skye could sense that he really wanted her opinion. She spoke slowly, choosing her words carefully. "I think that she's very unhappy and—and that she misses her mother a lot. And . . ." She hesitated. "It's just—" She stopped again and then finished. "There seems to be some sort of . . . of constraint between the two of you. Something that undoubtedly hurts her, too." She looked at him warily. Had she gone too far? She was, after all, an outsider.

He let out a long breath and nodded. "Maybe," he said finally, "I should tell you the whole story."

"Are you sure you want to?" Skye asked. "I mean, you hardly know me."

He looked at her intently. "I know you saved my daughter's life. I saw how you tried to protect her from what you thought was my anger. And," he added, "I watched for a minute from the doorway tonight when you read to her. I think," he continued softly, his eyes fixed on hers, "that, somehow, you need each other."

The sharp tears that filled her eyes were as unexpected as his words. Skye blinked rapidly and drew a deep breath. How had he come to see that so easily?

"Will you listen?" he asked.

Skye nodded.

"My wife and I separated when Karin was about three," he began candidly. "Karin stayed with her mother." He stared into the fire and spoke the bare facts in flat tones. "Debbie married again and moved to California. I didn't see Karin again for over two years. Debbie and her husband were killed on a Los Angeles freeway and I brought Karin home. That was nearly three months ago. She still avoids me."

"She was away from you for nearly half her lifetime," Skye said. "Maybe she just needs more time to adjust."

He shook his head. "I think there's more to it than that. From what I've been able to piece together, it seems Karin spent most of her time with an assortment of baby-sitters. To the point of neglect," he added bitterly and then exploded. "God damn it! Debbie knew how much I wanted Karin with me all along! She couldn't even be bothered to look after my daughter properly!"

Skye saw guilt mingled with the anger in his eyes. The modern family tragedy, she thought sadly. A wrecked marriage with the child caught helplessly in the middle. "Couldn't you have taken her?"

Bjorn's eyes were stony. "I didn't know how bad it was. Debbie convinced me that Karin had grown very close to Wade and that visiting me would just confuse and upset her. So, like a fool, I trusted her and stayed away instead of insisting we work it out.''

''I—I don't think you should be telling me all this,'' Skye protested uneasily. ''What can I possibly do? Maybe a psychologist—''

''Do you think I haven't thought of that?'' he interrupted harshly. ''She doesn't respond. She doesn't respond to anything. That day down by the lake—'' He stopped and ran agitated fingers through his hair. ''Depressed children often have...accidents,'' he said finally, his voice hollow.

It took a moment for the full meaning to sink in. ''No!'' she gasped. ''You can't mean—Bjorn, she's hardly more than a baby!''

He stared into the flames, his profile grim. ''Going down to the lake and climbing out on the ice like that was totally out of character. She's not an adventurous child. And suicide is more common among young children than is generally believed,'' he stressed. ''Many so-called accidental poisonings, accidents—well, they might not realize just what they're doing, but...'' His voice trailed off. ''We don't always realize the despair a young child can feel.''

Skye closed her eyes in momentary horror. One remembered the dreaded night she had stood on the edge of a Vancouver wharf hypnotized by the oily swell of the water, tired and utterly depressed, wanting nothing but release from her own private hell. She stared at the man in front of her, her eyes open wide now with compassion.

''We tend to equate a child's feelings with their stature,'' he said, holding her eyes. ''Karin's depression is every bit as powerful as...as yours was,'' he finished gently.

Shocked by his perception, Skye blinked and tore her eyes away from his. He had obviously seen something in her that she had thought she kept well hidden. Perhaps her emotional scars would never heal. She leaned forward, her elbows resting on her knees. What did he want from her, she wondered, rubbing her forehead wearily. She hardly knew him.

"I know we're virtually strangers, Skye," he said as if he'd read her thoughts. He watched her with an intentness she could feel. "But I—I've got no choice. Karin needs help, but no one has been able to get through to her."

"What makes you think I could?" She couldn't help but be touched by the appeal in his eyes.

"A feeling—just that, nothing more. She seems different with you—maybe because you saved her life, I don't know. But I think you could help her." His words were quietly spoken.

Skye shook her head, still uneasy about the idea. "What do you think I could possibly do that would help?"

"Just be her friend," he said. "Visit with her, either here or at the cottage. She goes to kindergarten every afternoon, but you could see her in the mornings or after four o'clock. And Skye," he added. "I'll pay you wages."

"Oh, no. Absolutely not!" Skye protested adamantly. "If you think I can help, I will, but not for money. I like Karin."

"I know you do, but I—"

"No money, Bjorn," she repeated with quiet determination.

He studied her for a moment and then nodded curtly. "Very well. But don't let it interfere with your painting or anything else. And let me know anytime you need a ride into Gimli—and if there's anything at all I can do for you, don't hesitate to ask.''

Skye nodded, a frown knitting her brow. Like it or not, she was committed. She knew that even if there was only a small chance that she could help Karin out of her depression, she had to try. The sad, lost look in the child's blue eyes tugged at her heartstrings.

She looked up to find another pair of blue eyes watching her closely. For a long moment she met his gaze, which hid none of his quiet concern. Skye's eyes swept down and she rubbed the rim of her glass with her finger nervously as she felt another kind of tug at her heart.

Skye left shortly after their talk, refusing Bjorn's persistent offer of a ride. With the dog at her side, she picked her way carefully along the dark shore, thinking about what she had agreed to do. Somehow, in spite of all her doubts, it felt right.

She remembered how a stranger had come to her aid when she desperately needed help and had no one to turn to. Often she wondered where she would be if it hadn't been for Theo.

She had left Reid the day after Jennifer's funeral. Stunned with grief, she had taken a bus across the country—from Ottawa to Vancouver. Her only conscious thought had been to get far away from Reid, fearing that if he found her, he might coerce her to return to him. Still frozen with shock, she had wandered through the unfamiliar city until she stood on the edge of a dark wharf, hunched over with despair, not thinking, not feeling, just utterly tired. A man, out walking his dog, had seen her and immediately sensed her despair. He had reached out and touched her shoulder.

"Are you all right?" he had asked with gruff concern. Skye had turned to him, seen the compassion in his eyes and had burst into tears.

That has been the start of a deep and lasting friendship. Theo's kindness and caring had helped her to start living again. A confirmed bachelor in his early forties, he had unselfishly shared his home with her until she felt ready to start out on her own. He had been there when she'd received the news of Reid's death, had assured her that she needn't feel guilt because she was relieved by the news. No, her feelings were perfectly normal, given the circumstances. Also a painter, Theo had encouraged her to take art courses at the university, adamant that she develop her talent. She made many friends through Theo—friends who helped to ease her loneliness.

Skye knew she could never repay him for his kindness. Not directly, anyway. But she could pass on to someone else what she learned from Theo. He would like that. Okay, she decided if she could help Karin, she would.

Sleep did not come easily that night. Skye curled up tightly in bed with no energy to get up and paint as she usually did when unhappy memories refused to be pushed aside. Well, she thought, sometimes she just had to let herself feel—however painful it might be.

She stretched out her legs and rolled over onto her back. Lacing her fingers behind her head, she stared into the darkness. Did a mother ever forget the feel of holding her firstborn in her arms, forget the soft, suckling mouth or the sweet, downy smell of babyhood? Skye caught her lip with sharp teeth and fought back tears. She was so tired of crying.

For nearly two years her life had been empty and aimless. The intense grief of Jennifer's death had slowly lessened, become manageable. Perhaps staying by the lake and involving herself with someone else's problems was just what she needed now. Bjorn and Karin might be strangers, but already she felt an affinity for them—both of them, she acknowledged, turning onto her side and hugging her knees to her chest.

The man was clearly hurt and puzzled by his daughter's withdrawal. Skye sensed that he was a private man by nature and knew how painful it must have been for him to ask a stranger for help. She saw his troubled face in her mind's eye, an expressionless mask that looked as though it was meant for smiles and laughter. Maybe by helping the child, she could help the man. She sighed softly in the darkness. She wanted to see him smile.

CHAPTER THREE

MORNING DAWNED CLEAR and warm once again. Skye was outside within minutes after waking.

The air was filled with the spicy scent of willow buds unfurling beneath the strengthening rays of the sun. Skye snapped a twig from one bush and rolled the sticky, bright green leaves between her fingers. She climbed the sandy rise to the lakeshore and looked around. There were only a few chunks of ice left from the slabs that had littered the shore and even they would soon disappear. She took a deep breath and grinned widely. It was a beautiful day.

Spring was always a delight but when it came to a land that had lain locked in the sterile grip of subzero temperatures for months on end, it was miraculous. Already it was impossible to believe that the immense lake that rolled as far as the eye could see had been completely frozen over, that Arctic winds had whipped snow across its surface into giant drifts along the shore. New green sprouted everywhere, and the birds were back from their sojourn south. The air seemed to tremble with the excitement of renewed life.

Spring was truly a season of change, Skye mused, sensing that a change was about to occur in her own life. On this clear vibrant day, she knew that the past, with all its sorrows, was falling slowly behind her. She turned her face to the sun, feeling the warming rays sink beneath her skin. Feeling light and happy, she ran down to the water and tossed in a piece of willow root.

"Get it, Bess," she ordered. The big black dog ran into the chilly water, splashing happily, chasing after the stick. There were still some chunks of ice around but Bess managed to stay clear of them.

"You're certainly in high spirits this morning."

Startled, Skye spun around. She stared for a moment and then grinned. "It's spring!" she exclaimed, noticing how attractive Bjorn's tall muscular form looked in his faded jeans and cotton shirt.

"It has been for a while," he said rather dryly.

"But today—" She shrugged. "I don't know. It's just . . . different, somehow."

He nodded. "Today we know it's here to stay."

"Exactly." She smiled, then turned to look out over the lake. "I like it here," she said and then jumped back with a squeal as the dog, stick in mouth, shook her shaggy fur free of water. "Bess, you great beast!" She took the stick from her. "Want to fetch it again?" A briskly wagging tail and a sharp bark answered her, and she tossed the stick back into the water.

"This could go on for hours. Bess loves the water, even when it's ice cold."

"She's been bred for it," Bjorn said. "Have you had her for long?"

"Almost two years." Skye smiled. "She was a gift from a friend—a very good friend," she added with the ready, warm feeling she always had at the thought of Theo. "He thought we'd take care of each other." She looked at Bjorn and grinned. "Actually he figured if I had to stop painting long enough to feed the dog, I might feed myself at the same time."

"Peanut butter sandwiches?" he jested and Skye was sure she saw the ghost of a smile. "I'm an awful cook," she admitted ruefully.

"In that case you'll have to eat with us more often." He didn't look at her as he spoke, but watched the dog paddling through the water.

"Oh, no—I couldn't possibly impose. Really, I manage just fine."

"I'm sure you do. But—" He paused and turned to look at her. "We don't really know each other, and yet I'm asking you to become involved in my problems. The least I can do is offer you a meal now and then and it will give us a chance to get better acquainted." He gave her a long pensive look that unnerved her slightly.

"Then the least I can do is accept—now and then." She grinned, trying to lighten the momentary tension, then knelt to pet the damp, panting dog, looking up at him from the corners of her eyes. "And, Bjorn. I'm glad you asked me . . . to help with Karin, I mean. I—I really want to."

He studied her wordlessly for a moment, his face shadowed by the sun. Finally he nodded as though satisfied. "I'll admit that was one of the reasons I came over. I wanted to be sure that you were sure. Walk back with me?" he asked suddenly. "Karin leaves for school in about an hour. You could have a bit of time with her."

Skye stood up, wiping her damp, sandy hands on her jeans. "I'd like that."

They walked along the shore, the dog running ahead of them. Skye felt at ease with the man beside her, silent though he might be. His request wasn't aggressive or threatening nor was he trying to score points. He was simply concerned with his daughter's well-being, and she could understand that.

"I'd like to see some of your paintings," he said unexpectedly as they neared the clearing that lead to his house. "I know someone in Gimli who might like to put them in her store for the tourist trade this summer."

Skye smiled. One way or another, he was going to return the favor she was doing him. "That would be nice," she said. "It'll beat hawking them in a parking lot."

He frowned at her flippancy. "That's how you make a living?"

"Yes. It's enough," she said. She saw no reason to tell him that she had more money than she would ever need.

When they arrived at the house, Karin was perched on a kitchen stool watching Mary roll out pastry.

"Hello," Skye said brightly. She included both of them in her greeting but her eyes were on Karin. "How are you today, Karin?" she asked, pulling out a stool and sitting beside her at the counter.

Karin ducked her head shyly. "Fine," she whispered.

"Good!" Skye touched the girl's shoulder lightly. "What kind of pie are you making, Mary?"

"Banana cream." Mary transferred the pastry to a pie plate. "It's Karin's favorite, isn't it, pet?" The child responded with a nod.

"I like it, too," Skye admitted.

"So do I." Bjorn had come up behind them.

Mary looked up at the three pairs of attentive eyes and laughed. "Save your drooling, gang—it's for supper."

Skye marveled at how comfortable she felt with these people. She sat on the stool chatting comfortably to Mary with occasional comments to Karin. Bjorn was watching and listening, saying little. She couldn't help but look his way.

His face intrigued her with those deep laugh lines that never laughed, but still somehow contradicted the hard set of his mouth and the shadowed look in his eyes. Those blue eyes! They drew hers like a magnet. She simply couldn't help looking at him. Was it just the artist in her that was intrigued?

His shoulders slouched against the side of the cupboard he was leaning on but she could see their width under the blue cotton shirt he wore. His hips were narrow, his legs long, and his jeans fitted with an alluring snugness. Her eyes lingered and then swept back to his face. He was watching her, one thick eyebrow quirked.

Skye smiled blithely. "I was trying to picture you hunched over a typewriter," she said easily.

His lips twitched. "And?"

She shook her head. "It'll have to be the Viking ship."

Skye noticed a definite softening of those firm lips and suddenly realized just how handsome and desirable a man he was. Surprised at the trickle of interest stirring within her, she looked quickly away, watching Mary slide pie shells into the oven.

Skye watched as Karin, silent as she always was, twisted a grubby piece of pastry with her fingers, making a shape, destroying it and starting again, the child's eyes glazed and staring somewhere distant.

A momentary panic touched Skye. What was she doing here? She didn't know these people. Why should she become involved in their lives? Maybe she should leave now while she still could, go back to her free-wheeling life on the road, far from all ties and encumbrances. She looked up from the small fingers that alternately shaped and crumbled the piece of dough.

Bjorn's eyes caught hers before she could look away, a silent plea in their depths. He had seen her indecision and was asking her to stay. Skye gave him a helpless, somewhat rueful smile. Of course she would stay.

Mary continued to move about the kitchen, seemingly involved in her tasks, but Skye knew from her quick, darting looks that she had missed nothing.

"Karin." Mary said, touching the thin shoulders. "It's time to go wash up for lunch. Take Skye with you and show her where the bathroom is." She smiled at Skye. "Bjorn was saying he'd like it if you'd take your meals with us."

Skye's fine dark eyebrows rose and she looked at him rather than Mary. "That would be nice," she said somewhat haughtily. "On occasion, perhaps."

"She doesn't want to impose, Mary," he drawled. "Either that or she prefers peanut butter sandwiches to your cooking."

Skye made a face at him as she stood up and reached for Karin's hand. "Come on, Karin," she said warmly. "Let's go get ready for lunch. You don't want to be late for school."

The child's sticky fingers curled trustingly in Skye's and she looked up with a shy smile. "I like peanut butter, too," she confided in her whispery voice as they left the kitchen.

Bjorn watched the door swing shut behind them. Mary saw hope in the eyes that had so often held despair.

"She'll be good for the girl, Bjorn," she said confidently. "You'll see." And she won't do you any harm, either, she added to herself. With a satisfied look, she began to set the table for lunch.

SKYE FOUND HERSELF falling into a comfortable routine over the following weeks. She would spend a good part of the morning with Karin, stay for lunch and then return to the cottage after she left for school. Bjorn was there to greet her and always joined them for lunch, but used the hours in between for his writing.

She was becoming very fond of Karin. The girl was still shy and withdrawn, but seemed to enjoy the time she spent with Skye, and obviously loved the dog. It was when she was with Bess that Skye caught glimpses of the happy, carefree child she should be.

Skye watched them one morning, a smile lighting her face as her nimble fingers filled in the figures on her sketch pad. It was a lovely day. The sky so immense reflected a soft blue onto the calm surface of the lake now free from ice and the sun pressed a delicious warmth onto her back. The new leaves were a vibrant green and everywhere birds cavorted with a freedom soon to be lost to the demands of hatching chicks.

A shadow fell across her paper. Startled, Skye looked up to find Bjorn standing beside her, watching his daughter at play. The sleeves of his cotton shirt were rolled up and his thumbs were hooked in the belt loops of his jeans. The sun glinted on his thick chestnut curls and again on the red-gold hairs on his arms. Skye slowly explored his lean length with her eyes, lingering on the taut thrust of his hips and the curve of his buttocks. An unexpected, warm feeling curled in the pit of her stomach and she looked quickly away.

It seemed ages before he finally moved. Still without speaking, he dropped lithely to sit cross-legged on the sand beside her. Skye turned to him with her ready smile.

"Finished writing?" she asked.

"I gave up. It's to hard to concentrate on a day like this. Actually," he confessed suddenly, "I'm finding it hard to concentrate, period. I feel as though my life has been on hold these past three months, like I'm getting nowhere fast—even my writing is suffering. I've started work on an adult book—one I've wanted to write for a long time, about a group of Viking settlers in North America before Columbus." He sighed and raked his fingers through his hair. "I know it's going to be good, if I could just start concentrating on it."

Skye nodded sympathetically, knowing the frustration that came when reality interfered with the creative urge. "It'll work out soon," she said. "Just give things a bit more time."

He nodded, his eyes now on Karin, then asked abruptly, "How does she seem to you, Skye?"

She followed his gaze to the child. "She seems quite relaxed with me, but..." She searched for the right words. "It's as though she's holding something back. Sometimes I feel like she's about to tell me something—" She gestured helplessly. "I just don't know, Bjorn. I wish I could do more."

He turned to her, one strong hand touching her arm. "You are helping," he said. "Look at her. She wasn't playing like that before."

"That's Bess's doing, not mine," Skye said ruefully, unconsciously rubbing her arm where his fingers had so briefly touched.

He shook his head. "It's not just the dog. She talks to Mary about you all the time—that is, when she does talk," he added bitterly.

"And you, Bjorn?" she asked quietly. "Does she tell you anything?"

"Not a damned thing!" The words were thick with underlying frustration. "I love that kid, Skye. She was such a bright and happy little girl before Debbie ran off with her."

"Why did she—" Skye stopped, realizing the question was none of her business.

"Why did she leave?" Bjorn finished, seemingly unperturbed. He was silent for a moment and then spoke tonelessly. "She wanted to live in a certain style, and in order to provide it, I had to work long and hard. So she became bored and restless. Wade came along with lots of money and a love for a good time." His lips twisted. "She was gone before I even knew we had a problem, taking Karin with her." He stared broodingly out over the water.

What had happened to Karin during those years? Skye wondered. Had she been mistreated or was her withdrawal a result of her mother's death and her unfamiliarity with her father? Whatever had happened, father and daughter needed each other very much, but were miles apart. Skye jabbed a stick into the sand and frowned. She wanted to help them, but how?

Bjorn looked at her. "When are the Siguardsons due back?"

"In a couple of weeks, I guess. I'm waiting to hear from them. They told me they usually come back about the middle of June, but would write and let me know."

"Where will you go then?"

"I don't know yet. I haven't made any definite plans. Maybe I'll find a place near here and park my van for the summer."

"This van of yours—is it a motor home?"

Skye smiled. "Hardly. It's a converted delivery truck, but it has all the comforts of home. Come to think of it, it is home." The words were carefree, but there was a hint of wistfulness in her voice.

"How long do you plan on leading a Gypsy life, Skye?"

She sighed. "I really don't know. Sometimes I come to a place and think, this is it—I could make a life for myself here, but ... the feeling never lasts. Sooner or later I want to go again."

He looked at her seriously. "What about here? Do you think you could stay around here for a while?"

"I ... yes, I think I could." She breathed deeply and looked around with appreciation. "I like it."

"Good," he answered as if satisfied with her reply, but he didn't elaborate. He stood up and brushed the sand from his jeans before offering her a hand.

"C'mon," he said. "Karin's got just enough time for lunch before the school bus comes."

Tentatively Skye put her hand into his and felt his grip tighten as he pulled her to her feet. He released it immediately and walked toward Karin and the dog. Skye gathered her sketching materials and followed slowly, conscious of the warm imprint his fingers left on hers.

Deciding not to return with them, she gave Karin a hug, telling her that she would see her the next day. Karin went with her father obediently, but her reluctance was obvious. Skye sighed and rubbed the dog's ears. She felt discouraged that there had been no change in the relationship between father and daughter.

She turned and trudged back to the cottage. Bjorn thought she could help them, but Skye was beginning to have her doubts. Karin was willing to spend time with her and seemed to enjoy herself, but was no closer to a reconciliation with her father.

Was it too late? Skye asked herself, sitting down on a lawn chair at the back of the cottage. Had those years away from Bjorn left scars too deep to ever really heal?

Skye, too, had been separated from her father at an early age, but the circumstances had been very different. Almost immediately after her mother's death, Skye had been sent away to an isolated boarding school north of Ottawa. Her father could have hired the best of housekeepers to help him raise his only child, but he had not wanted to even look at his young daughter, who reminded him so much of his late wife. She had been treated kindly and with affection at the school, but she'd never got over that uncomfortable and lonely feeling of having been rejected. Her father's visits had been limited to Christmas and one short week in the late spring before she'd be sent to summer camp.

Skye rubbed the back of her neck. She had long ago resolved her anger over her father's actions, but there were still times when she felt a pang of regret for what might have been, especially after he died. She pulled a twig from a willow bush and scraped at the soft bark. Maybe that's why she wanted to help Bjorn so much. He was trying hard to help his daughter and she admired him for it. It was more than her father had ever done for her. Or Reid for Jennifer, she thought bitterly. The twig snapped in half and she threw it down.

Reid might have been a more attentive father if Jennifer had been the son he'd always wanted. As it was, the contempt he had for women in general had carried over to his infant daughter and he had barely acknowledged her. Even her death had hardly touched him.

But then, she thought stonily, nothing ever really touched Reid. He had been a cold and unfeeling man, who she'd come to realize, had married her because, as her father's partner in a law firm and executor of his will, he had known exactly what she was worth.

Years of social isolation had left her relatively naive and trusting when it came to men. She had foolishly fallen for Reid's calculated wooing, thrilled that the handsome, older man wanted her. Starry-eyed, she had married him days after her nineteenth birthday. His charade of love and tenderness ended after the wedding.

Skye bit her lip and stared unseeingly around the tree-lined yard. Most women remembered their wedding night with pleasure. For her it had been an initiation in pain and humiliation. It was during sex that Reid's dislike of women was most apparent.

He had taken her coldly, without tenderness or passion, then when it was over he had stood at the foot of the bed, staring at her with a look of distaste, his thin lips curled in a sneer. "That was wonderful, darling," he'd said with calculated cruelty and walked out of the room to shower.

That first encounter had set the pattern. Once or twice a week he would use her in the same way, and though the pain eventually stopped, the humiliation never had.

He hadn't wanted her love. He'd just wanted someone he could shape and control. Subdued and more than a little frightened by the cold, hard man she had married, Skye let herself be molded into a model wife. They had staff who took care of the household tasks, so that Skye had time to keep herself immaculately groomed to Reid's tastes, and to be the perfect hostess at his parties while he paved the road to a political career. Whenever she could, she escaped to an unused corner of the basement and painted—something Reid disapproved of.

Her first moment of happiness in her marriage had come when she discovered she was pregnant. She'd wanted the baby more than anything she had ever wanted in her life and she became absorbed in her pregnancy—it was a kind of outlet just as her painting had been. Reid, pleased with himself at the prospect of a child to complete his carefully contrived family picture, left her alone. Jennifer's birth was relatively easy and nothing could diminish Skye's joy—not even Reid's disgust that she had given him a daughter, not a son.

Skye put her feet up on the edge of the chair and hugged her knees to her chest. For five months she had been happy. Jennifer had filled her life with love. She bit a trembling lip and dropped her head to her knees, remembering again the horror of bending over the crib one morning and realizing that her healthy, happy baby had died in her sleep. Jennifer's death had ultimately given her the strength to leave Reid, but she would have endured a thousand lifetimes with him if it would have meant her baby daughter's life.

Bjorn rounded the corner of the cottage and was about to call a greeting, but he stopped, seeing the despair in the huddled figure. He wanted to comfort her, yet hesitated, knowing instinctively that she wouldn't want him to see her like this—it was a private grief. He watched as her shoulders heaved in a long, shuddering sigh. She's so young, he thought, to have such pain. It was obvious, from the shadowed look that came too often to her eyes, that she had loved her husband deeply.

He went quietly around to the front of the cottage and knocked loudly on the door, "Skye?" he called, "Are you there?"

Skye was startled at the sound of his voice and pulled herself together quickly. She wiped her eyes and blew her nose, hoping the signs of her distress weren't too obvious. She went around to the front of the cottage and managed to smile.

"You caught me napping," she said easily. "I was snoozing out back. Did Karin get off to school all right?"

"Yes, she did," Bjorn replied. "Listen—I came to see if you wanted to go into Gimli with me this afternoon. I talked to Helga Johansson—she owns the gift shop I was telling you about, and she's interested in looking at your paintings. If they'll fit into the car, we can take some of them in with us."

"They should fit—most of my canvasses are small. It's easier for packing. Come in and help me pick a few."

"I suppose the local landscapes will sell best," she said, moving several paintings from where they were stored in a corner of the room, lining them up for inspection.

Bjorn examined them closely. "You know," he said finally, a note of genuine admiration in his voice, "you're really very good. Why don't you try for a hanging in a real gallery—a show. You'd make a lot more money."

"Maybe someday," Skye said. "It might be fun. But I'm still learning, still experimenting. I don't even know what type of painting I'm best at—landscapes, portraits, nature studies. Besides, it's kind of nice to know people buy them because they like them and aren't speculating on my future as an artist. You know—buying them on the chance that I'll become famous, then selling them for a profit."

"Isn't that the aim of every artist? To become famous?"

"I don't know," Skye said, "I just know I like to paint and if someone wants to buy something I've done, that's fine with me. Now, which ones do we take?"

"I like this one—and this one," Bjorn said, picking up two landscapes without hesitation. "And definitely the one of the moon over the lake at break-up. You caught that shadowed blueness of the moonlight on ice so beautifully. Oh, and the silhouette of the oak tree against the sunset—that's one of my favorite prairie scenes."

He pulled out another canvas, smaller than the rest, and looked at it thoughtfully. It was a portrait of a man with graying hair and a full, bushy beard, his brown eyes wide and smiling. "Is this your husband?" he asked hesitatingly.

"No—no," Skye answered quickly. "That's Theo, a friend of mine." She took the painting from him and separated it from the others. "He's the one who gave me Bess." She smiled, her voice warm with affection.

Bjorn looked at her closely for a moment, then turned his attention back to the rest of the paintings, quickly choosing three more.

"There," he said. "That'll give Helga an idea of what you've got. I think they'll sell fast. Can you be ready to leave in an hour?"

"Sure—easily."

"Good. I'll go back to the house and bring the car round. See you in a bit." He left quickly.

Skye stripped for a fast shower. She was glad that he had come over before her bout of depression had settled in. Sometimes it lasted for days. It came less frequently now, and was not as intense, but was still debilitating. Bjorn and Karin were proving a welcome distraction.

She thought about them as she shampooed her hair. She liked them both a lot. Karin, so frail and innocent, needing desperately to feel loved. And Bjorn... She closed her eyes and raised her head to the spray, feeling the shampoo slip down her body as new, exciting emotions stirred deep within.

She got out of the shower and dried quickly. Her choice of clothing was limited, but there was one pair of jeans that were still fairly new looking. She tucked in a crisp, white cotton shirt and rolled the sleeves up. Her hair, still damp, was combed straight back and tied with a red silk scarf. After sliding her feet into white sandals, she went to get the paintings ready.

Skye sat cross-legged under a spreading peachleaf willow waiting for Bjorn. The dog lay beside her, panting softly.

"You'll have to stay, Bess, old girl," Skye murmured as she heard the car approach, and guided the dog back into the cabin.

Bjorn parked and got out to help. They laid the paintings carefully on the back seat, padding them with blankets.

"All set?" he asked.

"Yep. Let's go."

The drive into Gimli was relaxed this time. They were becoming friends.

"How long has your family lived around here, Bjorn?" Skye turned slightly in her seat, wanting to hear him talk.

"For three generations now. My grandparents came here with their families at an early age—a few years after the first wave of settlers from Iceland."

"Why did people decide to leave Iceland?" she asked with interest.

"Well," Bjorn said thoughtfully, "I guess the main reason was a volcanic eruption in Iceland in 1875 which covered much of the land in one area with ash. Faced with the threat of starvation, a lot of people decided to emigrate. The first colony here was called Nyja Island— New Iceland—and was actually a separate republic for a while. Gimli was the first town established. Gimli is the name of the place in an Icelandic legend where the Norse gods were to be taken at the end of the world, a place where they would have eternal peace and happiness. Unfortunately," he continued with a sideways glance at her, "it wasn't true for some of the settlers. Many died that first winter from lack of good food, and later from a smallpox epidemic. Luckily most of them made it, and more Icelanders continued to emigrate in the years that followed. They learned to fish, even through the ice in winter, and once the land was cleared, many became successful farmers."

"That's interesting," Skye said. "I don't remember learning any of that in my history lessons."

"A peculiarity of Canadians," Bjorn said wryly. "We're taught the history of other countries, especially our neighbors to the south, and manage to learn only the bare facts about our own country. I've done most of my learning through research for my writing."

"Tell me more," Skye said, "About the Icelanders."

"Well, they were very literary people. Every home had books—in fact, one of the first things the settlers did was publish a little newspaper. The children were taught at home until they settled in Canada. Then they were sent to school to learn English, but Icelandic was still taught in the home. Of course, like many immigrants, they were gradually assimilated and few of the recent generations can speak Icelandic. But there is still a strong sense of culture and many of the traditions live on. Every summer there is an Icelandic Festival called the *Islendingadagurinn*, which means the day of the Icelanders."

Skye enjoyed listening to him. His deep, expressive voice gave her a warm, comfortable feeling. And it wasn't often that she heard him say much at all.

When they reached Gimli, he drove down the main street and parked near the wharf, the cluster of small fishing boats in full view. Helga's shop had a combination of books and gifts, and she was delighted with Skye's paintings. They discussed prices and commission over a cup of coffee, and Skye promised to bring in more of her work in the next couple of weeks. Helga was anxious to have lots of her paintings as tourists and cottage owners were beginning to arrive for the summer and it was the best time for sales.

While Bjorn tended to a few errands, Skye went to see about her van. It had been fixed, but the mechanic had his doubts as to how much longer the motor would last. It was just too old. It would probably be good only for short trips, he told her, but its days of chugging across the continent were over.

Skye looked at the van—her home for so many months—wondering what she should do with it. Selling it would be like parting with an old friend, but that was probably the most practical thing she could do.

"Do you think you could sell it?" she asked the mechanic.

"Maybe," he said with mild enthusiasm. "I know a couple of guys might want it for hunting trips. Should hold up pretty good for that."

"Tell you what," Skye said. "Get the best deal you can for me and twenty percent is yours."

"You got yourself a deal, lady. Should sell pretty quick. You need a ride anywhere?"

"I have one, thanks, but I could use a box or two. I might as well take what's left inside."

Skye quickly packed the few remaining odds and ends that she'd left in the van into the boxes the mechanic had found for her and took one last look around with a little pang of regret. The makeshift home had served her well.

She sat on one of the boxes outside the garage waiting for Bjorn. She knew she'd need some kind of vehicle soon. Perhaps this time she'd buy a car—a new one, and a trailer for times when she felt the urge to get on the road again. Money was no problem. Her father, a successful lawyer and astute investor, had left her well provided for, though Reid had made no provision for her in his own will.

She saw Bjorn coming and stood up to wave. "I sold my van," she told him, putting the boxes on the back seat of his car. "At least, I put it up for sale."

Bjorn was frowning as she got in beside him. "Why?"

"Phil—the mechanic—told me it wouldn't hold up for any more long trips," she explained. "He thought he knew someone who may want it for hunting trips, so I thought I might as well get rid of it while it's still worth something."

"What are you going to do now?" he asked, turning onto the highway.

"Buy something newer. Maybe a mini-van—something with lots of room for Bess. I can always buy a trailer later on."

"But— Listen, Skye, I know this is none of my business, but can you afford it? I mean, you aren't exactly earning a steady income."

"I've got money in the bank," she said carelessly. "And selling paintings by the roadside is more profitable than it sounds." She grinned. "Low overhead."

"You realize you're without any transportation at all now," his tone was curt. He was a little put off by her carefree attitude.

"No, I'm not." She smiled charmingly. "I happen to have a very kind neighbor who would love to take me car shopping."

His lips twitched and he looked at her, shaking his head. "I guess you do at that," he said. "When do you want to start?"

"Actually, if you take me to where I can catch a bus into Winnipeg that would be enough. I thought I could stay for a day or two and see what I can find."

"When would you like to go?"

She shrugged. "I'm in no hurry."

They drove in silence for a few miles. Bjorn's brow was knitted as though he was deep in thought and Skye was content to sit back and watch the fields roll by.

"Skye," he said finally, with a sideways glance. "Have you heard from the Siguardsons yet?"

"Oh—yes. I got a letter yesterday, actually. They aren't coming here this summer, after all—they decided to go and stay with their son and daughter-in-law in Edmonton. So they've rented the cottage instead. Someone will be taking it over in a few weeks. It's too bad they aren't coming," she added. "I was looking forward to seeing them again."

"So I guess you're going to have to leave."

"That's right." Over the past few weeks, leaving was something she'd thought of less and less.

"But after today," he said with a quick look at her through narrowed eyes, "You've got no way of leaving."

She twisted around in her seat to look at him. "I realize that, but I'm not too concerned. It'll work out."

"Well, what I want to suggest is that you come and stay with us for a while."

"Oh, I don't think so, Bjorn," she said quickly, feeling her heart give a little skip of excitement. "I couldn't do that."

"Why not? Karin would love it. So would Mary."

"What about you, Bjorn?" she asked bluntly. "It's your house."

He turned to look at her, his eyes twinkling. A slow smile spread across his face and all his lines fell beautifully into place. "Actually," he drawled, "You're kind of interesting to have around. I think I could put up with you."

Skye's gaze was fixed on his smile. It was everything she had thought it would be and more. Devastating, she thought, dazzling.

"Well?"

She gave her head a little shake. "It's for Karin, isn't it?" she asked, not deluding herself. "You still think I can do her some good."

"Yes, it's for Karin's sake," he agreed quietly, his face serious again. "I know you're good for her."

Skye sighed. "I don't know, Bjorn. I—"

"Have you any other plans?" he interrupted.

She shook her head. "No—none."

"Then what do you have to lose? You'll have a roof over your head, meals—I even have a room where you can set up your easel."

Skye was silent. What did she have to lose? She stole a sideways glance at him. Except her fragile peace of mind—her heart? Oh, she could lose all right, but . . .

"What do you say, Skye?"

"Bjorn—are you sure about this?"

He gave her a quick sincere look. "Absolutely."

"Then my answer is yes—on one condition."

"And what's that?"

She grinned at him. "You have to promise to smile at least once a day. You have a beautiful smile, Bjorn. You should display it more often."

He stared at her and chuckled. "It's a deal," he said. He reached across the seat and squeezed her fingers in his. "Thank you, Skye."

"Thank you," she corrected, still feeling the pressure of his fingers when he removed his hand. "You're doing me a favor."

"I have a feeling you'll be doing me a bigger favor, Skye," he said softly. "Much bigger."

Skye frowned and turned to look out the window. He seemed convinced that she could help Karin, that she could help bridge the gap between father and daughter. Was that all he wanted from her?

CHAPTER FOUR

IT DIDN'T TAKE SKYE LONG to move as she had only a few possessions. Bjorn had suggested she move in with them right away and Skye saw no reason why she shouldn't. She tried to ignore a niggling feeling she had on moving day that it might be best to buy a new vehicle and be off. Perhaps she was becoming too involved in their lives, at a time when she wasn't ready for involvement.

Everyone seemed to be glad she'd decided to stay. Mary welcomed Skye in her usual friendly, down-to-earth manner, and Karin seemed quite content that she'd arrived. And Bjorn—she knew exactly why he had invited her into his home. It had a little to do with gratitude and a lot to do with hope. She had no illusions. He saw her only in terms of what she might be able to do to help his daughter.

There was a bedroom for her upstairs next to Karin's, just down the hall from Mary's. Done in soft greens and white, it was bright and cheerful. Pretty white lace curtains hung from the corner window which looked out over the yard to the lake beyond.

"The bathroom is across the hall," Mary said. "You'll have to share it with Karin and me. Bjorn has his own, off his room. Come with me," she continued. "I'll show you his room. It's in the new part of the house."

Bjorn's room was separated from the other bedrooms by a hallway and a short flight of stairs. It was
huge, but comfortable looking, decorated in an attractive blend of earth tones—browns and beiges mostly.
His desk and typewriter were in an alcove with shelves
of books on either side, a carved wooden screen sepa-
rating it from the rest of the room. On the far wall,
French doors opened onto a small deck with a pan-
oramic view of the yards and lake.

"And the bathroom," Mary said, gesturing toward
the connecting door. "You've got to see that!"

It was an ultramodern bathroom. A huge, whirlpool
tub with carpeted steps leading up to it dominated the
room. A small bay window was home to a jungle of
plants, and the smoked glass windows gave the room a
soft glow.

Skye's eyes widened and she looked around with
pleasure. "Wow!" She grinned. "How—"

"Sybaritic," Bjorn finished dryly, coming up behind them, Karin by his side. "My sister's idea of the
height of luxury. She included it as a surprise—I
thought I was getting a sink and a shower. That tub
came as quite a shock."

"So you don't use it?"

"Actually," he drawled, "I've found it to be an
amazing source of inspiration for writing. Every author should have one."

Skye had a sudden vision of him lazing in the tub,
bubbles clinging to his chest and shoulders as he sipped
from a glass of wine, and of herself sitting opposite, her
legs entwined with his. The image was vivid and arousing and she could feel her cheeks flush. She looked
quickly away from him.

"It would probably have the same effect on an artist," he went on, completely unaware of her discomfort. "Feel free to use it anytime. That door over there connects with the hallway. Just sling a towel over the doorknob and I'll know you're in there."

"There are plenty of towels in the cupboard," Mary volunteered, pinching a dead leaf from one of the plants. "And there is always plenty of hot water. Now, Skye, why don't you go and unpack before lunch. It'll be ready in about twenty minutes."

"Okay," Skye said, forcing aside thoughts of her and Bjorn sharing a bath. She turned to Karin, who stood silently by her side and held out her hand. "Come with me, Karin. You can help me if you want."

"'Kay," the little girl whispered and slipped her cold, thin hand into Skye's. She raised her head and smiled shyly.

Skye returned the smile and then, as they turned to go, gave the same smile to Bjorn, but he was watching his daughter, his face once more locked in a hard, unreadable expression.

Skye awoke the next morning to the sound of the soft creak of her bedroom door slowly opening. She lay quietly watching as Karin's curly head poked cautiously into the room. Then the rest of her, clad in pink pajamas, followed. Skye watched through her lashes, hiding a smile as the little girl tiptoed to the edge of the bed and peered anxiously at her face.

Skye opened her eyes suddenly and with a quick move, grabbed Karin around the waist and swung her onto the bed. The child squealed with surprise and then giggled as Skye rolled her over, tickling her ribs.

"I came to see if you was awake," Karin said, her eyes bright with laughter.

"Well—am I?" Skye demanded, tickling her again.

"Yes!" she squealed and dissolved into more giggles.

Bjorn stuck his head into the room, his eyes sparkling at the sound of his daughter's laughter. "Hey!" he said playfully. "What's all the noise in here?" He crossed the room to the foot of the bed.

The laughter fled from Karin's face, and was replaced by a blank, withdrawn look. She edged to the side of the bed and swung her feet back and forth, staring intently at the rhythmic motion.

Skye watched the enthusiasm fade from Bjorn's face, saw his hands clench in frustration as he turned on his heel and left the room.

Skye sighed and reached out to touch Karin's rigid back. "Why don't you go get dressed, sweetie," she suggested gently, "while I go take a shower. Or do you need help?"

Karin shook her head. "No," she whispered, her eyes downcast as she slid off the bed and started for the door.

"Hey—come and give me a hug first," Skye said, holding out her arms. With the slightest hesitation Karin came and Skye folded her arms around her. "Mmmm," she murmured against the child's silken curls, "that makes me feel good. Away you go now, kiddo," she said with a final squeeze. "Come back when you're finished dressing and you can help me make my bed before we go downstairs."

Skye pushed back the covers and reached for her old terry robe. With all the unexpected company in her bedroom this morning, she was glad she'd decided to wear her oversize T-shirt to bed. It might be short, but it covered her well enough. Not that Bjorn was likely to notice one way or another, she thought ruefully. Belting the robe around her waist, she went to shower.

Karin was tugging at the covers on the bed when Skye returned to the room. "I made my bed," she said.

"That's wonderful. Won't Mary be surprised?" Skye dressed quickly in her favorite yellow shorts and a white T-shirt, combed her hair and tied it back while it was still manageable.

"Okay, Karin—let's get this bed finished and then we'll go down for breakfast." Skye tucked in the sheet and fluffed the pillows. "What do you usually have for breakfast, Karin?"

"Cereal. But not the kind my—the kind I used to eat. Mary says I have to eat healthy stuff so's I can grow big and not get sick."

"Good for Mary." Skye had never heard Karin offer her so much information.

Mary was working away in the bright, cheerful kitchen, Bess sitting close by and watching her every move, when Skye and Karin came in.

"Good morning, Mary," Skye said. "I hope Bess hasn't been a bother."

"Never," Mary said with a decisive shake of her head. "I love dogs and this one is special. Well mannered, too."

Karin slipped her hand from Skye's and went straight to the dog. "Hi, Bessie," she said, patting the animal's big black head. Bess responded with a swipe of her tongue, the feathery tail thumping on the tiled floor.

"What do you want for breakfast, Skye?" Mary asked.

"Just coffee, please."

Mary gave a huge sigh. "Not another one. No one around here wants to eat in the morning," she complained mildly.

"I'll have a piece of toast if it'll make you feel better," Skye said with a grin.

"How about an omelet?" Mary suggested.

Skye shook her head quickly. "No, thank you. I couldn't—really."

Mary lifted her shoulders in resignation. "Toast it is." She turned to Karin. "Come on, pet. Give those hands a wash and come eat your breakfast."

"She says you make her eat healthy stuff," Skye said with a smile, watching Karin pull a stool to the sink so she could reach the tap.

"She pointed out her usual brand to me one day in the grocery store," Mary said in a low voice. "One of those dreadfully sweet kinds—with marshmallows in it yet! Imagine letting a child eat candy for breakfast— that's what it amounts to. She said she had it for lunch sometimes, too." Mary's nurturing instincts were clearly horrified, and she shook her head. "The poor little thing was so thin and sickly looking when Bjorn brought her here that it just about broke my heart."

Skye wanted to ask questions, but Karin had finished at the sink and was returning the stool to its place along the wall. As soon as she found a private moment with Mary, she'd ask her what she knew about the child's past.

Karin ate quickly, drank her orange juice and then jumped down, taking her bowl and glass to the counter beside the dishwasher.

"Karin—why don't you take Bess out to play in the yard while Skye finishes her coffee," Mary suggested.

"'Kay," she said willingly, heading for the door. "C'mon, Bessie," she called. "Want to play chasing sticks?"

"Where's Bjorn?" Skye asked as Mary refilled their coffee cups.

"Writing," Mary answered. "Or at least trying to. From the look on his face this morning, I'd say he's probably pacing the floor instead. Did something happen?"

Skye stirred sugar into her coffee. "Karin came into my room this morning. I was tickling her and she was laughing. Until she saw her father." She sighed. "Her mood changed instantly. She became all withdrawn and...and sullen again. I don't know what's wrong, Mary. If she was a few years older, I'd say she was doing it on purpose, trying to get back at him for what she might have seen as his rejection. As it is, I think she was too young to even really remember him properly. Has she ever talked to you about it?"

Mary shook her head. "Never. And any direct questions are met with a shrug and 'Don' know.' Oh, she's sweet and biddable enough, but she's closed part of herself off and nobody has been able to get her to talk. We really don't know much about what life was like for her."

"Tell me what you can, Mary." Skye knew that if she wanted to ever get through to Karin she had to explore all avenues, not only for the child's sake, but for Bjorn's, as well. They needed each other—Skye knew that.

Mary poured them more coffee and leaned forward, elbows resting on the countertop. "From what Bjorn has been able to piece together, Debbie and her new husband partied almost nonstop—they were always off jet-setting somewhere or other. Karin, poor thing, was left with baby-sitters. For some reason, the sitter never wanted to return and there was always someone new. The last one was barely sixteen and more interested in entertaining her boyfriend than in caring for Karin. It seems Karin spent most of her time watching TV and staying out of the way. You know she wasn't even enrolled in school before Bjorn brought her here!''

Skye frowned disturbed by Mary's words. "It doesn't make sense, does it, Mary? Why would the woman take Karin and then neglect to take proper care of her? If she didn't want the bother, surely it would have been easier to leave her with Bjorn.''

"Who knows the reasons?'' Mary said. "Maybe it had something to do with the child support—quite a bit, from what Bjorn told me. And Debbie was rather immature and selfish, from what I understand.''

Skye felt a rush of resentment toward the dead woman whose inconsiderate and selfish actions had left two people who needed each other poles apart and hurting badly. She tilted her cup and swirled the dregs of coffee around the bottom, wondering if she could possibly help to mend the rift.

SKYE FITTED EASILY into her new routine. School was over for the summer, Karin was always around and being together was an enjoyable experience. They helped Mary around the house, weeded the flower gardens and went for long walks along the sandy lakeshore, stopping to talk to cottagers and as the days passed, Karin became more dear to her.

And so did Bjorn. Though he spent little time with them during the days, Skye always felt the presence of the big, gentle man watching over them. Whenever he could, in his quiet, unobtrusive way, he joined them, never seeming to resent the love and ease with which Karin responded to her. Rather he seemed hopeful, as though some of Karin's affection might spill over to him.

Both of them touched her heart, but Bjorn, she had to admit, did more than that. She was growing more aware of him physically—his strong, very male presence filling her senses. She had felt so sterile and lifeless for so long. It was wonderful just to feel again and to know she could.

But Bjorn showed no signs of returning her feelings. He treated her with a friendly gratitude and not much more. He was relaxed with her, unaware of the emotions she was finding harder and harder to hide. He had little time for her; all his attention was focused on his daughter, which was understandable.

So much about the man appealed to her, and she wished that he'd devote some of the attention to her. Even his books, children's stories though they were, thrilled her. His writing was clear and colorful, conveying a strong sense of adventure and she knew the book he was working on would be a hit. She had looked up one night from reading one of his books and saw his handsome figure standing by the living room window staring out into the moon-lit yard and knew, with a start of surprise, that she was falling in love.

SKYE STRETCHED LAZILY on her beach towel, then sat up to look out over the lake. She loved the prairie summers. The days were long and hot, making the beach the perfect place to be. Karin sat near the water, carefully packing sand into a bucket, making another turret for the sand castle she was building. Beyond, on the blue, sparkling surface of the lake, sailboats glided by, bright multicolored sails puffing out lazily in the breeze. Huge white pelicans caught the updraft and spiraled upward to soar high above the water.

Skye knew the instant Bjorn was beside her, and she smiled up at him. "Another gorgeous day."

He sat down on the sand beside her. "Exactly how summer should be," he said. "Long, hot, lazy days." He leaned back on his elbows and looked around with pleasure. "Who could ask for anything more?"

I could, Skye thought wryly, casting a glance at him. His summer wardrobe consisted almost entirely of cut-off jeans, slung low on the hips, snug and faded. Sometimes he'd add a cotton shirt and fasten it carelessly with a button or two, but that did little to hide his superb body.

Her glance turned into a lingering look. She had long ago quit telling herself that her attraction was purely out of artistic interest. He might have made a magnificent model, but the last thing she felt like doing was taking out her paints. No, she wanted to touch him, to feel the sun's heat on his muscular shoulders and back. She wanted to run her fingers over the tanned smoothness of his chest and feel his arms close around her.

She looked quickly away and shut her eyes, trying to stem the rush of desire for him. How much longer could she hide her feelings?

She looked at her body, tanned a deep, golden brown and covered only by a tiny, bright orange bikini and thought wistfully that her normally sparsely clad body never seemed to draw even a second glance from him. Was it only because his attention was focused on Karin or was he just not interested? She stifled a sigh of resignation. Not interested was the depressing message she got from him.

"Karin really enjoys the beach," he said, watching his daughter turn her bucket upside down and release the latest turret.

Skye smiled. "She does. When she gets that castle finished, she'll call Bess and the two of them will run through it until it's all flattened. She thinks it's hilarious. They do it over and over again."

"She's much happier since you came, Skye," he said.

"She seems to be," she agreed. "I just wish . . . well, that things were better between you, Bjorn."

"It'll come," he said quietly. "It has to. At least now she laughs and plays—she even looks healthier. That's a lot to be thankful for." He fell silent as he watched Karin with a longing that made Skye wish she could do more for him.

She turned to stretch out on her stomach, resting her head on the crook of her arm.

"Would you like me to rub some lotion on your back?"

Skye peeped from the shelter of her arms, her eyes widening in surprise. "I . . . yes, if you don't mind. My skin is getting quite dry. I had a lot of sun over the winter, as well."

"Which explains why you're so brown already." Bjorn removed the top from the bottle of suntan lotion, squeezed some on to his hands and rubbed them together. He laid his palms on her shoulders and then began light, rhythmic strokes, stopping to undo the tiny back strap of her bikini top.

There was nothing perfunctory about his touch. His hands moved in leisurely unison from her shoulders to the small of her back, rubbing in the lotion and swell-

ing her attraction to him into a tide of yearning. Then
he started on her legs. He did each ankle and calf in
turn, then moved with one slow, easy stroke from the
backs of her knees, over the smooth length of her
thighs, to the bottom of her bathing suit.

It could have been a lover's touch. Skye wanted to
look at his face to read what might be there, but she
dared not move. Her body slowly tensed under his
hands and she fought to keep it still, to stem the quiv-
ering desire that mounted in slow, exquisite waves. She
wanted to roll over and hold out her arms to him, to feel
his lips crush against hers, wanted him to stretch out
beside her and cover her body with his. If they had been
alone, she might have dared.

"There—that ought to do." Bjorn's hands stopped
their magic touch. He refastened her top, gave it a teasing snap and leaned back down on the sand.

Skye bit back a moan of frustration. She wanted to
look at him, but knew if he saw her face, she would give
herself away. If what she was feeling was as one-sided
as she was afraid it was, it would be very awkward and
embarrassing for both of them.

"Hey—did you fall asleep?" he asked after a few
moments of silence.

"Mmmm—just about," she lied, her voice husky.
She turned over and sat up, hugging her knees to her
chest. "That was very...relaxing."

One shaggy eyebrow quirked as he searched her face.
"It was? I thought..." His voice trailed off as he looked
up the beach. "Here's Mary," he said with surprise.

Mary, in colorful Bermuda shorts, was trudging
across the sand barefoot, picnic basket in hand. "Hi!"
she called cheerfully. "Isn't it a lovely day?"

Karin and Bess ran from the water to greet her, and Bjorn leaped up to take the basket.

"Thanks, Bjorn," Mary said. "I thought a picnic would be nice for lunch." She sat on the sand beside Skye. "My friend Maggie phoned to say she's visiting with her sister. I'm meeting them for supper and then we're going to bingo. I'll leave something out for supper," she added to Bjorn.

"I'll make something," Skye volunteered. "At least," she amended with a grin, "I'll try to make something."

"What?" Bjorn asked. "Peanut butter sandwiches?"

Skye made a face at him. "Maybe—and if you're lucky, I'll even toast the bread."

"Oh—burnt peanut butter sandwiches," he nodded knowingly, his eyes twinkling.

Mary laughed. "Well, don't worry about supper yet. Let's eat lunch first. Here, Karin, give me a hand spreading out the cloth. Are you hungry?"

Karin nodded. "An' so's Bessie."

"Well, then," Mary said, "it's a good thing I brought her a bone, isn't it?"

They ate cold chicken and potato salad, washing it down with icy lemonade. The dog gnawed contentedly on her bone and gulped down scraps of chicken handed to her by Karin.

Skye nibbled abstractedly. What had Bjorn been going to say before he saw Mary? Had he found the whole thing as arousing as she had? She stole quick glances at him, but his face was as impassive as ever except when he looked at his daughter. Then she would catch a glimpse of the hurt and frustration he carried within him. She poked dejectedly at her salad. Until he had Karin back, there would be no time in his life for anything or anyone. And even if he did have the time, he would probably never love her.

SKYE AND KARIN WERE BUSY in the kitchen when Bjorn came in after writing for most of the afternoon.

"What's for supper?" he asked, leaning on the counter.

"Well," began Skye, slicing a tomato and adding to lettuce in a wooden bowl, "I thought veal scallopini would be nice, but—"

"But?"

She grinned. "Mary said there were frozen pizzas in the freezer, and *those* I know how to cook!"

Bjorn chuckled. "I gather your husband must have done all the cooking. Either that or you ate out a lot!"

Skye's face instantly stilled and she turned away without comment. With an expressionless voice, she asked Karin to get a bottle of dressing from the fridge, thinking about Bjorn's casual comment. There had never been any moments of joy, of amusement, in her marriage, but how did she go about letting him know that?

She wasn't proud of the way she had cowered in that intolerable relationship, unable to leave a man she hated. It was a time in her life she didn't like to talk about.

After supper, Bjorn suggested that the three of them take a walk along the lake. Skye agreed readily, wanting to shake the unpleasant mood that had settled over her.

"Karin," she said as she scraped the plates for the dishwasher, "Could you please get me a T-shirt from my room?" She wanted to put it over her halter top.

"There's a blue one in the second drawer from the bottom."

Karin went willingly and was back in minutes carrying the T-shirt and something else as well. "Skye," she said, "I found this picture, too. Who's this little baby?"

"Karin!" Bjorn admonished, taking one look at Skye's stricken face. "You shouldn't have touched that."

"No, Bjorn. It's all right. It's my fault. It was in the drawer with the T-shirts." She spoke calmly, but her voice felt hollow and distant. "That...that's Jennifer, Karin. My little girl."

"Where is she?" the child asked, frowning intently. "Did you go away and leave her?"

"No, sweetie. She...she died." Skye groped behind herself for a chair and sat down heavily. Karin came and stood beside her, still staring at the picture.

"You must have felt real bad," she said, rubbing a finger over the glass as Skye so often did. "Like I did when..."

"When your mother died?" Skye asked gently.

Karin frowned. "No," she said slowly. "Like when my—" She stopped abruptly with a sideways scowl at Bjorn.

"When what?" Skye asked. When your father left you? she wanted to say.

Karin's lips pressed together. "Nothin'." She looked down.

"Tell me, Karin," Skye said, motioning to Bjorn not to say anything.

"I forget," Karin said, kicking a toe against the chair leg.

"Come on, sweetheart," Skye coaxed, rubbing her small back gently. "You know you can tell me. When did you feel that bad?"

"I forget," Karin repeated with a shrug, sliding away from the chair. "I'm going to see if Bessie wants to go for a walk."

Skye looked at Bjorn and raised her hands helplessly. She could see conflicting emotions come across his face. He clearly felt sympathy for his daughter but also seemed anxious to know what Karin was holding back. She wished she could help Bjorn, but she didn't want to push the child for fear of making matters worse. She'd tell them when she was ready.

Bjorn glanced at the child, noticing she still held the picture in her hand. "Karin," he called. "Before you leave, would you please put that picture back where you found it."

"It's okay," Skye said quickly. "I'll do it. I have to go upstairs for a moment anyway." She smiled shakily and left the room, conscious that Bjorn was watching her closely. She knew that if Karin had left the room, he would have started questioning her. Gently, perhaps, but she knew all the questions well and hated them. How had Jennifer died? With your husband? People always asked. They saw it as a double tragedy, but it wasn't. Reid's death held no sorrow for her.

She went upstairs and laid the picture back among the clothes and shut the drawer. She wasn't hiding it. She simply didn't want to look at it all the time and be reminded each and every day of her little Jennifer. After sitting on the bed for a few minutes to compose herself, she went back downstairs, trying to appear cheerful.

"Okay," she said with forced enthusiasm. "I'm ready for that walk, if you are."

Karin clung to Skye during the walk with unusual intensity, pointedly ignoring Bjorn except for the odd angry look she threw in his direction. Maybe her anger was a good thing, Skye reflected, watching the child—perhaps the start of the healing process. If Karin felt anger, then it was a healthy sign if she expressed it. But the combination of the child's mood and Bjorn's brooding presence, his hooded, sidelong glances at them, made for a tension-filled evening. By the time they had returned to the house, Skye's head ached unbearably.

She tried to hurry Karin to bed, but it took the child a seemingly endless time to relax. Finding out about Jennifer had wound the child up like a top. As soon as they were alone, she began to question Skye about the little girl in the picture. She seemed fascinated that Skye had had a daughter and she wanted to hear all about it over and over again. Skye wasn't sure how to approach the situation but she answered all her questions and let her talk herself out. She didn't feel up to talking about Jennifer. All she wanted was for Karin to settle down so she could escape to the quiet darkness of her room.

SKYE KNELT ON THE FLOOR by the window in her room, resting her arms on the sill. She stared through the screen at the deepening gloom as a thick, black cloud drowned the lingering twilight, turning the air thick and humid.

The house was quiet. Mary had returned from her bingo game some time before. She had talked to Bjorn for a while and then they had gone to their rooms. Mary was probably watching TV. What was Bjorn doing, she wondered.

Skye found she was thinking about him almost constantly. She felt such sympathy for him, but growing stronger daily was her awareness of him as a man. She sighed and rubbed the tight muscles in her neck. His touch this afternoon on the beach, unexpectedly sensual, had fanned her desires, making it hard to conceal how he made her feel.

Bjorn—surely he must have felt something. He had done more than rub the lotion into her skin. He had caressed her with those lean, sensitive fingers. How could something she had felt so intensely have been one-sided? She sighed again and stirred restlessly. She might have been a wife for two years, but she'd never learned about men's desires.

The air grew close as the storm approached. Thunder rumbled restlessly, and lightning pulsed within the statelike confines of the cloud. A sudden gush of wind splashed raindrops against the screen. Lightning split the cloud, lighting the yard for an instant of purple-white clarity, followed by a reverberant crack of thunder as darkness fell again. Rain dropped in earnest.

Like all summer storms, it hit with fury and then left as fast as it had come. Lightning flickered sullenly as the grumble of thunder grew distant. The wind stilled and a half moon climbed the eastern sky, trailing its light across the rippled surface of the lake.

Skye left her room and slipped quietly down the darkened stairs to the back door. Easing it shut behind her, she stood for a moment on the porch steps, breathing the moist, cooled air deep into her lungs. She ran down the steps and across the wet grass to the swing tied to the gnarled branches of an ancient oak tree and sat on the damp seat. Giving herself a little push, she raised her face as the notched leaves rustled and released cooling drops of captured rain. She gripped the knotted rope tightly and pushed again, harder, her long, bare legs pumping her higher as she leaned back, arching over the ground with her feet pointed toward the moon half-hidden by swaying branches.

Bjorn watched from the doorway. He wasn't surprised that she hadn't been able to sleep. She had tried to hide her feelings with that bright smile and easy chatter, but he could tell how forced her cheerfulness had been. He was beginning to realize a lot of things about this woman. He knew that her sadness never really left her—and how could it? Not only did she have to adjust to the loss of a loving husband, but to her infant daughter, as well. The tragedy touched him deeply.

He watched as she slowed herself down, the arc diminished until she gradually stopped. She sat unmoving, her head against her shoulder. He went outside quickly, crossed the lawn and stood in front of her.

"Skye—are you all right?"

She raised her head and forced a smile, her face white in the pale moonlight. "I'm fine," she said, surprised to see him. "I just felt the need for some fresh air."

He reached out with a gentle hand and touched the moisture on her cheek. "Tell me about her, Skye," he said softly. "Tell me about Jennifer."

Her eyes shut against the new rush of tears. "She was so sweet, Bjorn," Skye murmured brokenly. "So happy—she was always smiling, laughing in her baby way."

"What happened?" he asked gently.

"I—I woke up one morning—it was late. I'd slept in. Usually she would have had me up..." Skye blinked back tears. "I knew something was wrong, I just knew. I went to her room and . . . and she looked like she was asleep, but she wouldn't wake up. I shook her, screamed at her, but . . . she wouldn't wake up." Tears coursed down Skye's cheeks and she shuddered violently. "Oh, Bjorn—she was . . . cold. So very, very cold."

Bjorn pulled her from the swing and wrapped his arms around her in sympathy. "Oh, Skye," he murmured against her hair. "I'm so sorry."

She clung to him wordlessly for a moment and then looked up with a shaky smile. "I'm sorry. I'm usually okay. It's just—"

He smiled gently. "Karin took you by surprise."

She nodded and tried to step back. "I—I'm all right now, Bjorn," she whispered, pushing her palms lightly against his chest.

"No, you're not," he said, holding tight. "You're wet and probably chilled. Come into the house and I'll fix you a hot drink." He kept an arm around her shoulders as he guided her back.

He flicked on the stove's overhead light but left the rest of the kitchen in darkness. Skye was grateful not to have to face his scrutiny under the harsh glare of fluorescent light.

"Cocoa?" he asked.

She nodded, sitting on a stool at the breakfast counter. Shivering, she wrapped her arms around herself. Her hair was curled into ringlets around her face and the T-shirt she wore as a nightgown was pasted to the curves of her body.

Bjorn put two mugs of milk into the microwave oven and then looked at her with a frown. Quickly he went into the laundry room which was just off the kitchen and brought back a fluffy bath towel. He was about to hand it to her, but instead shook out the folds and used a corner to gently wipe her face dry. He rubbed her hair into a drying, dusky cloud and then draped the towel over her shoulders, his eyes lingering on the thrust of her nipples under the clinging material.

"You should get out of that," he said roughly. "It's damp."

"I—I will," Skye said with a touch of embarrassment. "Before I go to bed."

"Skye . . ."

She looked up shyly, her eyes questioning.

He curled a finger under her chin and tilted her face up toward his. Their eyes were locked for a moment then his lips touched hers, so soft and giving. Skye sat perfectly still, her eyes closing as she savored their incredible softness. With a tiny sigh, she pressed closer, returning the kiss, her fingers resting on his shoulders before curling into a caress.

As her lips sparked beneath his, he wrapped his arms around her in an explosion of sensation and pulled her to her feet. Instantly their bodies clung together and he groaned at the soft, convulsive thrust of hers, stroking his hands over her back to cup her hips. He felt the tingle of a moan as her lips parted under his and he kissed her deeply.

A sudden, shockingly loud ping from the microwave sent them flying apart to stare startled around the kitchen and then back at each other, both of them wide-eyed and breathing heavily.

"Saved by the bell," Bjorn murmured, his eyes twinkling. He touched her shoulder lightly and turned to take the mugs from the oven. "Cocoa's ready."

Skye took her cup and sat down heavily, her mind and body still caught in the magic of his kiss. It was all she'd dreamed it would be and more, so very much more. She glanced at him over the rim of her cup.

His eyes met hers, a rueful look in their blue depths. "Skye," he said. "I never meant for that to happen."

Skye looked down and nodded. She knew that. He had kissed her in sympathy and for comfort. But perhaps now that he knew what it could be like... She looked up and smiled. "That's okay. And...and I'm not cold anymore."

Bjorn relaxed with a chuckle. "The cocoa—right?"

She nodded solemnly. "Right."

They finished their drinks in silence. Bjorn rinsed out the mugs and Skye dried them and put them away.

"Do you think you can sleep now?" Bjorn asked.

"I think so." Skye smiled. If anything kept her awake, it would be the lingering memory of his kiss and the hope that there would be another. "Good night, Bjorn."

He caught her shoulders before she could leave and held her while he dropped a kiss on the side of her mouth. "Good night, Skye," he whispered. "Sleep well."

He leaned back against the counter watching her go, his eyes lingering on the curve of her hips and the smooth length of tanned leg beneath her short white nightgown. He made a sudden move as if to follow, stopped and shook his head, turning slowly away.

Skye lay in bed, hovering between sleep and consciousness, reliving Bjorn's kiss. In her dreamlike state, the kiss was but a prelude to deeper, more passionate caresses, a continuation of his sun-soaked touches on the sand. An intense longing rushed over her and she rolled onto her stomach, moaning softly into the pillow, wishing she dared slip down the hall to his room and turn her dreams into reality.

CHAPTER FIVE

SKYE SAT CROSS-LEGGED in the middle of the garden, lazily picking the first of the peas for Mary. She felt the hot, humid air rise like a blanket around her as the sun drew last night's rain from the black soil. She snapped a pod from the vine, feeling languid and content. Her own personal storm had dissipated and she felt okay again, maybe for a little longer this time.

Her growing feelings for Bjorn helped distract her from dwelling on the past. She smiled softly, reaching for another pod as she remembered how delightful his hands had felt on her heated skin as he rubbed in the suntan lotion, his touch like a lover's caress. And last night's kiss, lingering and arousing, drawing her desire for him closer to the surface, making it impossible to deny. Had he noticed the effect he had on her? Did he care? Would anything change because of that kiss?

She frowned and tucked a dark curl behind her ear. She didn't feel very optimistic. He had never really given her occasion to believe he was interested in her as a woman. As far as he was concerned, she was here for Karin. If she wanted to stay, without causing embarrassment to herself—or to him—she'd do best to remember that.

She heard him come up behind her. Turning, she looked up past long, muscular legs with their sprinkling of red-gold curls, past lean hips in faded, cutoff jeans, over a smooth golden chest half-covered with a carelessly buttoned shirt, and smiled into eyes as blue as the summer sky above her. "Hi," she said, tossing a pea pod into the bowl beside her.

"Hi, yourself," he said, squatting. "Is that all you've picked?"

Skye peered into the bowl and grinned. "What do I know about picking peas? Are you here to help?"

"If we expect to eat peas today, I guess I'd better," he drawled, his long fingers searching the vine for plump and rounded pods. "Didn't you ever have to pick peas as a kid?"

Skye shook her head. "It's not a requirement of boarding schools or summer camps."

Shaggy chestnut brows quirked. "What—no home with a backyard garden?"

"No," she sighed. "I had a deprived childhood. Actually," she corrected, "it wasn't bad. Different from most, but I learned to cope. There were always lots of interesting people around, always something going on. Now you, I take it—" she pointed with her chin to the rapidly filling bowl "—served your pea picking apprenticeship."

"That—and planting, hoeing weeds and picking potato bugs from the plants...everything. Before we moved to Toronto, that is."

"Did you hate to leave?" she asked curiously.

"Yes." He looked up over the garden to the wide horizons. "I belong here. I always knew I'd come back. It was easier for Lara—and my mother had family in Toronto. For her, it was the right move to make after my father died."

When they finished picking peas, they moved onto the porch steps outside the kitchen to do the shelling.

Mary sent Karin out to help. Skye patted the space between her and Bjorn, but Karin pointedly ignored
Skye's invitation to sit between them and instead
squeezed onto the edge of the step next to Skye. Skye
glanced at Bjorn, saw his eyes darken, and the still,
shadowed look settle on his face. Their easy chatter was
gone and they finished the task in silence.

Skye looked from father to daughter with concern,
wanting desperately for things to be right between them.
She hoped the anger Karin had started to show toward
Bjorn the night before was the breakthrough they had
been looking for. It had to be healthier than her usual
flinching withdrawal. Once Karin had acted out her resentment at Bjorn for what she saw as his abandon-
ment, maybe she would feel free to love him again.

Skye looked at Bjorn's silent face again with a throb
of longing. If he got Karin back, she wondered wistfully, would he have time for her?

After lunch Bjorn disappeared to his room and Skye
decided to do some work, too.

"Karin," Skye said, "I'm going to do some painting. Would you like to try?"

"Okay," Karin said enthusiastically. "I like painting!"

Skye smiled and held out her hand for Karin. She
hadn't done much painting since she'd moved in, but
she drew whenever she had a free moment. Many of the
sketches would be the basis for future paintings, but
most of them she drew for fun and relaxation.

She did her painting in a small room off the kitchen,
which Mary also used for sewing. It was bright, with
windows on both the north and east walls, furnished
only with Mary's sewing machine, two chairs and,
along one wall, a large, sturdy oak table.

Skye pulled a chair to the table and laid out paper and paints for Karin. "There you go, Karin," she said, dropping an old T-shirt of Bjorn's over the girl's head. "What are you going to paint?"

"Bessie," she answered, dipping a brush in the jar of water and then rubbing it on a cube of paint. "Chasing sticks in the water."

"Okay, Kar—go to it," Skye said, thinking wryly that it seemed the child responded to the dog more than anyone. It was easy to love animals. They accepted the love, returned it and never made demands.

Skye sat on a chair near one of the windows. It was open and a soft breeze eased through the screen bringing with it a sweet, floral scent. She picked up her sketch pad and began to draw Karin as the child worked studiously on her painting.

"There," the young girl said finally. "Come see, Skye."

Skye put down her pad and went over to the table. "Oh—that's great, Karin! It's so colorful—and look at that silly dog splashing in the water! That's good work, lovey." She squeezed her thin shoulders affectionately. "Give it a minute to dry and then run to show your father."

Karin folded her arms across her chest and stuck out her lower lip. "No!"

Skye's eyebrows rose in surprise. That was by far the harshest tone she had ever heard Karin use. "Why not?" she asked.

The blue eyes narrowed and the curly head shook mutinously. "Don' want to," she muttered.

"But Karin..." Skye began, hurting for Bjorn. "Your daddy would love to see such a beautiful painting."

She glared at Skye. "He's...he's...he's not my daddy!" she burst out. "My daddy's dead, like your little girl."

"Wha— Oh no, Karin!" Skye was stunned. "Who told you that?" Bjorn not her father—was that what she thought? "Who told you that?" she asked again in a quieter voice.

Karin hunched her shoulders in a shrug.

"C'mon, honey," Skye coaxed gently. "You can tell me."

The blue eyes filled with tears. "Once when I was very little, I cried and cried 'cause I wanted to see my daddy and Wade got mad an...and—" she sniffled "—he said I couldn't 'cause doncha know he's dead and he was my father now and to stop crying or he'd give me another spanking!" She ended the rush of words on a hicupping sob.

Skye closed her eyes in horror. "Oh Karrie, Karrie— that isn't true, sweetheart. It isn't true. Wade lied to you." She scooped the girl into her arms and held her close, rocking back and forth. "Bjorn is your daddy— your real daddy. I promise you." How could that man have said such a horrible thing?

"Karin," she murmured, looking at the tear-stained face. "What...what did your mother say when Wade told you that?"

"Nothin'. She was out. She was always out. She didn't love my daddy anymore," she added sadly.

Debbie was always out, just as Bjorn had told her. She was constantly leaving her daughter with uncaring baby-sitters or a man who spanked and lied callously to the child, Skye thought bitterly, when all the time Bjorn would have been overjoyed to have Karin returned to him. What kind of woman had she been? Had she ever realized the lie Wade told Karin? Surely she would never have condoned it.

Skye carried Karin to the chair in the corner of the room and sat down. "Karin—do you believe me? That Bjorn is your father?"

Karin burrowed her face on Skye's chest, her shoulders rounding in a shrug and she began to cry.

"He is, lovey," Skye murmured into the silky curls as she rocked back and forth. "Why, as soon as I saw him, I knew. He didn't even have to tell me—I could see it. Your eyes are exactly the same color as his—blue like the sky outside this window. And your hair is just like his, too, all curly and kind of red." She patted her thin, trembling back. "And I remember when he told me about when you were a baby and how much he loved you. He wanted to keep you with him when he and your mother couldn't live together anymore, but he thought you'd be happier living with your mother—and he loved you so much he wanted you to be happy, even if it meant he'd be lonely for you and miss you. He didn't know you were unhappy, darling, really he didn't."

Skye couldn't tell if she was taking any of this in. Would she believe her right away or was it going to take time to undo all the damage that had been done? She rested her cheek against the soft curls. At least now they knew where to begin.

She sat rocking Karin until her arms ached, whispering to her about her father and how much he loved her, how much he had missed her. Finally Skye could feel her little body relax and as she gave a shuddering sigh, the tears stopped. She was asleep.

Slowly Skye got up. Sleep was probably the best thing for Karin right now, and it would give Skye time to talk to Bjorn. She passed a startled Mary in the kitchen and mouthed a silent "Later" before going quickly to Karin's room. Gently she laid the girl on the bed and pulled the comforter from one side to cover her. She stared compassionately at the flushed, tear-stained face and then left to find Bjorn.

He was in his room, working at his desk. There was a sheet of paper in the typewriter and a crumbled pile on the floor near the wastepaper basket. She knocked on the partially opened door and he turned and looked at her in surprise.

"What is it?" he asked.

Skye sat down on the edge of the bed and looked straight at him, her eyes troubled. "I've been talking to Karin," she began, and quickly told him what she had learned.

Bjorn's face was slack with disbelief by the time she had finished. It slowly darkened with anger and he slammed a fist on the surface of the desk.

"What kind of man would tell a lie like that to a child!" He jumped up and paced the floor. "And Debbie...!" He bit off an expletive, kicking savagely at the papers on the floor. "Where the hell was she when all this was going on?" He stopped his pacing abruptly and looked at Skye. "Where's Karin?"

"In bed. She fell asleep after...after she stopped crying. I told her the truth, Bjorn, but I don't know if she took it in."

He nodded, the lines deep in his face. "Skye, could you sit with her in case she wakes up? I've got to make a phone call." He was reaching for the phone on the night table beside his bed.

Puzzled, Skye went to Karin's room. She wondered who he could be calling? She sat carefully on the edge of the bed and tenderly watched the sleeping child. Poor little thing. Taken from her father, neglected, lied to...and then having to suffer through the death of her mother only to be taken in by a man she couldn't remember, a man who had to be a stranger because she believed her father to be dead. She would have been too young to have more than a hazy recollection of Bjorn. It would have been easy for her, feeling lonely and abandoned, to believe the lie she had been told. Skye brushed a stray curl back from Karin's sticky cheek. No wonder she had been so silent and withdrawn, afraid to communicate anything but her most basic needs.

"Skye." Bjorn spoke softly and beckoned from the doorway.

Skye went quickly and they sat on the top stair near Karin's door.

"I talked to my friend, Dave Rosen," Bjorn explained, his voice controlled and matter-of-fact. "He's a child psychologist with one of the school divisions in Winnipeg. He's seen Karin a few times. He says not to rush her, that it may take some time for her to really believe that I *am* her father. He suggested that I should dig out some pictures taken when we were still together. Show them to her when she wakes up." He ran his fingers through his hair and jumped up. "Stay with her, Skye. Please," he added absently. "Bring her to me when she wakes up. I'm going to look for those pictures now."

It was almost half an hour before Karin woke up.

"Hi, lovey," Skye said with a cheerful smile and a quick hug. "That sure looked like a good sleep. Come on—let's go wash your hands and face."

Skye chatted casually, making no remarks about the pictures. When they had finished washing, she took Karin's hand and led her downstairs. "Let's go see what your daddy is doing,'' she said. Her only reaction was a quick sidelong glance at Skye.

Bjorn was sitting on the couch in the living room, looking through an album. He turned when he heard them come into the room and smiled. ''Hey, Karin, I found some pictures of you and me and your mother. Bring Skye over and we'll look at them.''

The album was filled with the usual collection of family snapshots taken at Christmas and on birthdays. Karin was rapt. She turned the pages slowly, examining each photo thoroughly, her glances at Bjorn becoming longer and more open. The last picture had been taken on Karin's third birthday as she sat on a shiny new tricycle.

''I 'member that bike!'' she exclaimed suddenly and then ducked her head shyly as if taken aback by the excitement in her voice.

Bjorn touched her shoulder briefly. ''And I remember how fast you used to ride up and down the sidewalk. I used to call you Speedy.''

Karin gave a little nod and smiled as though she, too, remembered.

Karin finished going through the album and the rest of the day sped by with an undercurrent of excitement. Skye had told Mary what had happened and she listened along with Skye and Karin as Bjorn casually talked about his home in Toronto, mentioning things that Karin might remember and telling her about things she had done as a baby. Karin said little, but listened intently, her eyes no longer shuttered and expressionless when she looked at Bjorn, but round with curiosity and hope.

At bedtime she turned her head away shyly when Bjorn kissed her good-night, but it was a long way from the rejecting flinch of the night before.

Skye bathed Karin as had become her custom and tucked her into bed. As she read her a bedtime story, she realized with a pang that soon it would be Bjorn who'd be doing this not her. That was how it should be Skye admitted to herself, but it meant that soon she would be gone from their lives. There would be no reason to stay.

She closed the book and turned out the bedside light, stooping to kiss a soft, round cheek. "Good night, sweetheart."

"Night," Karin murmured, snuggling under the covers. Her eyes opened suddenly and danced with hope. "Y'know," she confided in a whisper, "I think ... I think he really might be my daddy."

Skye stroked the soft curls so like Bjorn's. "He is, Karrie, and he's very happy to have you here because he loves you a lot. Sleep now."

When Skye went downstairs Bjorn was waiting for her in the living room. "Did she say anything?"

"Not much—but she's beginning to believe the truth. She wants to, but she's being cautious."

Mary came in from the kitchen. "Well, how is she?"

"Asleep," Skye answered. "And I believe she'll be okay. She just needs time to adjust."

Mary was pleased. "That's wonderful. I knew you'd be good for her, Skye."

"It was nothing I did," Skye disclaimed. "She just happened to blurt out what was bothering her."

"No," Bjorn disagreed quietly. "She wanted to tell you. I'm sure of it. Dave had always felt she was holding something back, but he couldn't get it out of her—and he's an expert at getting kids to talk. I phoned him again just now," he said. "And he suggested that I bring Karin in to see him this weekend. He and his wife, Miri, are friends of mine," he explained to Skye. "I often stay with them when I go into Winnipeg. So, Mary, can you hold down the fort this weekend?"

"No problem. It'll give me time to get some of those peas in the freezer."

"I'll help," Skye volunteered.

"Uh-uh." Bjorn shook his head. "You're coming with us. Dave and Miri are anxious to meet you, and it'll be a good time for you to start looking for a new car."

So she could leave, she thought with a feeling of reluctance. "Are you sure I won't be intruding?"

"Never, as far as I'm concerned," he said, his eyes soft and sincere as they held hers. "And Miri was adamant that I bring you."

Skye felt her cheeks flush and looked away quickly. "Mary, do you mind keeping Bess?"

Mary shook her head. "I like having her around. Well, you two," she added, "I'm going to go put my feet up in front of the TV." She yawned. "That was a wild time in the old bingo hall last night. Maggie really gets things going. Good night," she called as she left the room.

"Good night, Mary," Skye and Bjorn chorused.

"I think I'll take Bess for a walk," Skye said.

"Mind if I come, too?" Bjorn asked, standing up and stretching lithely.

"Not at all." Skye watched him with covert pleasure. He was wearing jeans and a white cotton shirt with the sleeves rolled over his arms. He looked as virile and as handsome as ever, but there was something different about him. His face had lost its set look of undefined pain, and his eyes were no longer still and guarded. He seemed, somehow, infinitely more attractive and she was already captivated. How much deeper could her feeling grow?

It was dark along the shore, but the milky way gleamed like diamond dust in the inky, velvet sky. They walked along the dim strip of white sand, the lake a quiet murmur in the still darkness. The dog loped ahead, invisible.

"Let's sit for a while," Bjorn suggested.

Skye sat beside him, her shoulder lightly touching his. She sifted the fine, cool sand between her fingers and looked out over the lake, awed by the immensity of the night sky.

"Skye?"

"Mmm?"

"Thank you," he said simply, finding her hand and holding it. "I know it's still going to take me time with Karin, but at least now I know where to begin. I owe you a lot, Skye."

"No," she protested uneasily. She didn't want gratitude from him. "You owe me nothing, Bjorn."

His fingers tightened on hers. "I do, you know. I had thought of a hundred reasons why Karin might have resented me—but that she thought I was an imposter— that her real father was dead!" He fell silent for a moment.

"It was an awful, helpless feeling," he said finally, "not being able to get through to her, and feeling guilty because she had every right to hate me. I did desert her, leave her with a mother who didn't really care. If I'd bothered to check just once instead of taking Debbie's word for everything..." He sighed. "Now, for the first time in a long while, I feel hopeful, as if I have a chance with her. I really love that girl, Skye," he admitted gruffly. "I'd do anything for her."

Skye squeezed his fingers in silent understanding. "I know." Her voice was soft.

They sat for a while, then walked back to the house, a silent bond between them.

"I'm going to bed," Skye said when they entered the living room. "Good night, Bjorn."

Bjorn put his hands on her shoulders and turned her around to face him. He touched her lips softly with his. "Thank you," he said again.

Skye had closed her eyes at the jolt of sensation. She opened them quickly when his lips left hers after too brief a stay and stared at him for a moment before managing a smile. "Good night again," she whispered with a tinge of sadness. Turning away from his bright, observant eyes, she went upstairs.

She lay awake for a long time thinking about how empty her life would be without him. Rolling over onto her side, she sighed softly and searched for a cool spot on the pillow. She knew she'd have to leave soon. All she wanted was to enjoy her newfound feelings of love, to give it freely and to have his love in return.

CHAPTER SIX

EARLY FRIDAY MORNING they left for Winnipeg. Bjorn took the scenic route along the lake, which was lined with countless cottages. The day was bright and clear, already hot. The miles rolled by in comfortable silence.

Skye kept glancing at Bjorn and Karin. Both of them seemed more relaxed than they had ever been. Karin was still shy around her father, but she was starting to respond positively to him and, given time, they would form a strong, loving relationship, Skye believed.

But where did she stand with them—with Bjorn? She had accomplished what he'd wanted. Did he expect her to leave so they could get on with their lives? He had given her no sign that he had any feelings that went beyond friendship and gratitude. She grimaced. She leaned her head against the car window and stared at the road ahead. It was obvious that he liked her—and becoming equally obvious that like was all there was to it.

It grew hotter as they approached the jagged skyline of the city. Heat steamed from the pavement and was reflected from brick and concrete walls, surrounding them uncomfortably. Skye plucked at her jeans and wished she had worn something cooler.

"It's not far now," Bjorn said. They had driven through the downtown district to a quieter residential area. Elm trees lined the boulevards in a long arch providing cool shade for the streets.

"Good," Skye replied. "I'm hot," she complained mildly.

Bjorn glanced at her, his blue eyes widening. "We should be able to remedy that soon enough," he drawled.

Skye looked at him, her suspicion aroused by his teasing tone of voice, but his face gave nothing away. He pulled into the driveway of a big, ranch-style house with a brick front and a large, tree-lined yard.

"Here we are," he said. "Leave the suitcases. I'll bring them in later. Karin," he added, "could you carry Skye's purse for her?"

Skye handed her purse to the willing child, wondering what he was up to.

"I'm sure they're in the backyard on a day like this," he said, leading the way. "Let's go round and see." He ushered them through a gate at the side of the house, closed it carefully behind them and then grabbed Skye by the shoulders.

"Wha—Bjorn! What are you doing?" Skye's voice rose indignantly as he scooped her up in his arms with an exaggerated wink at Karin. "Bjorn—put me down!"

"In a second," he said with a grin, his long legs taking them effortlessly around the side of the house to the backyard. "Hi, everyone," he called. "We're here. This," he said, pointing down with his chin, "is Skye."

Skye managed a smile, noticing the swimming pool. "Bjorn—you wouldn't!" She pushed against his chest and glared at him. "Bjorn—don't!"

"Hold that pretty little nose, sweetie," he jested, "while I do you a favor." He held her over the edge of the pool and unceremoniously dumped her in.

She came up sputtering, splashing water at him that he managed to dodge. "You—you!" she gasped, glaring at him as she swam to the side.

"Watch your language," he murmured, his eyes laughing. "There are children present."

Skye eyed him again then looked at the laughing woman sitting upright on a lawn chair beside the pool. "Does he get like this often?" Skye asked plaintively, pulling herself out of the water.

"Every once in a while," the woman answered with a smile. "I hope you plan on revenge."

"Hey—wait a minute, Miri," Bjorn protested. "The lady was hot. I was doing her a favor. Don't go giving her any ideas."

"I don't need any, Bjorn." Skye made a face at him. "I'm thinking them up all by myself."

"Attagirl." Miri laughed. "Rebecca," she added, turning to the teenage girl sitting beside her, "could you please get a towel?"

"Sure, Mom." The girl went off obligingly, a wide grin on her pretty, tanned face.

"I'm Miri, in case you haven't guessed," she said, turning back to Skye. "That was my daughter, Rebecca, and this is my son, Jeremy."

"I'm Skye Cameron. It's nice to meet you," she said, including them both in her smile. Miri was a short, slim woman with bright brown eyes and smooth black hair lightly sprinkled with gray. Jeremy looked about twelve, a wiry version of his mother.

"Karin," Miri said warmly. "It's nice to see you again. Do you remember Rebecca and Jeremy?" she asked as her daughter returned to the poolside.

Skye accepted a towel from Rebecca with a smile of thanks, turned to a grinning Bjorn and stuck out her tongue.

"Would you like to go change, Skye?" Miri asked.

Skye shook her head. "Not just yet. I think I'll dry off in the sun for a bit first." She sat in the chair beside Miri and patted her face dry. "Don't tell Bjorn," she said in a low voice, "but it felt kind of good."

Miri grinned in reply. "It also," she said quietly, "felt good to see him relaxed enough to do something like that."

"Hey!" Bjorn's voice broke through. "Are you two conspiring against me already? You could at least wait till Dave gets here to side with me. Where is he, anyway?"

"He had an appointment," Miri explained. "He should be back in about an hour."

"Good. That'll give me time for a swim. Come on, Karin," he said. "Let's go get those suitcases and change into our bathing suits. Same rooms, Miri?"

"Same rooms. Skye's in with Karin. Rebecca, maybe you could help Karin change."

"Okay, Mom." She got to her feet with a cheerful grin and followed Bjorn and Karin. Jeremy kept close behind.

"Listen," Miri said carefully. "I don't know if you and Bjorn are . . . well, I put you in separate rooms because of the kids, Rebecca especially. She doesn't miss a thing."

"Oh!" Skye blushed and then added as matter-of-factly as she could, "No, we're not . . . not involved that way. Karin and I became friends and he asked me to stay and help out with her. That's all."

"Well, from what Dave told me, you've done a lot for them."

"I'm just glad things are going to be all right," Skye said with sincerity.

"Me too. He's quite the man, isn't he?"

"Uh, I— Yes, he is. Have you known him long?"

"Since he moved back from Toronto. But he and Dave have been friends for several years. They met in university."

Skye nodded showing interest.

"So, Skye," Miri went on. "Tell me about yourself—where you're from, what you do, how you met Bjorn—things like that. I have an insatiable curiosity." Her brown eyes sparkled and she grinned. "Dave calls it nosey."

Skye chuckled and sat back comfortably, filling Miri in on some details. Not everything—she wanted to keep it light, and she hardly knew her.

They were still chatting when Bjorn came back with the kids. He and Karin had changed into bathing suits. Rebecca guided the child to the shallow end and Karin splashed happily. Skye stared at Bjorn as he stood, arms raised, on the edge of the diving board, his black trunks a brief interruption of his golden brown skin.

"Have you painted him yet?" Miri asked with a teasing smile, watching her face.

"A few thousand times," Skye admitted ruefully. "And maybe one of these days I'll get around to actually using paints and a canvas." She watched him knife neatly into the water, and then turned back to Miri. "I think I'll go change now," she said. "I'm dry enough not to drip all over your house."

"I'll show you your room," Miri said, standing up. "Hey, Bjorn! Can I get you anything?"

"A beer would taste pretty good right now," Bjorn said, swimming lazily to the side of the pool.

"I'll bring you one in a minute. I'm going to show Skye to her room first."

"Coming in for a swim, Skye?" he asked with a grin.

She dismissed him with a wave of her hand and followed Miri into the house, a smile tugging at her mouth. He's smiled so much this week, she thought with pleasure. It was there more often than not, lighting his eyes, waiting in the lines on his face, giving him an appealing, boyish charm. His face was made for smiles.

Miri's house was as neat as a pin and furnished in a comfortable style just right for children. She showed Skye the guest bedroom, which was bright and cheerful, with twin beds covered by rose-sprigged comforters. Her suitcase was at the foot of one bed.

"I hope Bjorn told you to bring something a bit dressy," Miri said. "We're going out tomorrow night."

"He didn't," Skye said. "But I wanted to do some shopping, anyway."

Miri's eyes lit up. "Great! I love shopping. You don't mind if I come along, do you?"

Skye laughed. "I was hoping you would want to. When can we go?"

"How about after supper? We usually eat early, and the stores are open late tonight. Dave and Bjorn will need some time to talk about Karin, anyway. What do you need?"

"Everything," Skye answered promptly. "Summer clothes—cotton skirts, tops, shoes, makeup. And," she added, patting her half-dried curls, "a haircut."

"We'll go downtown," Miri said, planning ahead. "There are some good department stores and lots of great dress shops. The haircut will have to wait until tomorrow. I'll phone my hairdresser and get her to squeeze you in. Now—you get changed and come back out to the patio. I'll have a cool drink waiting for you.''

What a kind woman, Skye reflected as she changed into her bathing suit, pulling shorts and a T-shirt over top. She had felt slightly apprehensive about staying with strangers, but after meeting Miri, she felt relaxed and was looking forward to the rest of the weekend.

She could hear shouts of laughter through the bedroom window. Resting her arms on the sill for a moment, she watched, smiling as Bjorn splashed in the pool with the kids and chuckled as Miri threatened to drop his bottle of beer in the water if he dared get her wet.

The change in Bjorn over the past months was incredible. She had been attracted to the dour, straightfaced man, and had felt compassion for the pain he suffered over Karin. But this new man emerging—the fun-loving, teasing individual was so attractive that merely looking at him made her heart beat faster. Turning away from the window, she picked up a comb and tugged it through her hair, meeting her eyes in the mirror with a rueful smile. She was head over heels in love with him.

They shared a bond of love for Karin, but was that all there was between them—all there would ever be? Skye put down her comb with a sigh. She should have been more wary about becoming so involved with them; the man and his daughter were woven firmly into her healing heart. If Bjorn couldn't return her love, she would lose both of them. She rubbed the frown lines that knotted her brow, thinking of the pain that would bring.

"REBECCA IS GOING to take Karin to the store down the street for some ice cream," Dave Rosen said as he closed the door to his den after dinner. He was a tall, thin man with a receding hairline and horn-rimmed glasses. He splashed Scotch into two glasses, handed one to Bjorn, and sat at his desk.

"She's going to be okay, Bjorn," he said, leaning back in his chair. "Kids are remarkably resilient and now that we've got to the root of the problem, she should bounce right back." He smiled at his friend and raised his glass to his mouth. "Just continue the TLC."

"An easy prescription," Bjorn insisted, pulling a chair up to the desk. "Can I expect any problems?" He sat down.

"It's possible that once she accepts you fully—starts feeling more secure—she'll test you a bit. Maybe get angry and act out her feelings. If that happens, just be calm, reassuring. She'll need to believe that she's safe with you and that it's going to last even if she's bad. Let her know that you love her and that you're glad she's with you no matter what. Bjorn, I'm sure she'll be all right."

"It's a relief, Dave," Bjorn said. "For a while there, it looked like nothing would change." He took a sip of his drink. "And it's thanks to Skye that it did."

"Skye," Dave said reflectively, watching him. "She seems like quite a woman. Know much about her?"

"No, not really. She doesn't say much about herself. I do know that she lost her husband and a child about two years ago." He stared thoughtfully into his drink. "How long does it take to get over something like that?"

Dave shrugged. "Depends. A husband—three or four years maybe before things start to come together, though it always depends on the individual. A child . . . that's something different." He leaned forward, elbows on his desk. "We expect to lose some people from our lives—parents, even spouses, though not until later in life. But our children are supposed to outlive us—kids simply aren't supposed to die. It's one hell of a shock when they do. And if, in her case, the husband and child died together, one death could be mixed up with the other."

Bjorn frowned and shook his head slowly. "I don't think it was like that. From what she told me about the baby, it sounded like crib death. She's never said anything about her husband."

"There's often a lot of guilt involved with SIDS—the sudden infant death syndrome," Dave explained. "Parents think that if only they'd checked on the baby, or woken up sooner. It's hard for them to understand that it wouldn't have made any difference." He looked closely at Bjorn. "All these questions—you interested in her?"

Bjorn flashed a wide grin. "Wouldn't you be?"

Dave laughed. "Miri would kill me—but, yes, I probably would be."

"Any advice?"

Dave frowned thoughtfully. "I don't know her well, but I noticed she still wears her wedding ring. To me that indicates that she hasn't come to terms with the marriage being over. Oh, she accepts her husband's death, I'm sure, but she could still feel married—or loyal—to him, if you understand what I mean. She'll have to have a real feeling of finality before she can take that ring off."

Bjorn took a sip of his Scotch and nodded mindfully.

THE SHOPPING TRIP was a complete success. Miri was fun to be with and had a good eye for clothing. For the first time in years, Skye enjoyed buying new clothes. She knew a lot of her enthusiasm was due to the fact that she wanted Bjorn to see her looking her best for once, and not like a scruffy, half-starved artist. By the time they had finished shopping, Skye's wardrobe had some great new additions.

Bjorn's reaction when he came in to say good-night to Karin and saw all the bags and boxes was unexpected. "Skye," he asked with a frown, "is this all your stuff?"

"All of it," she replied with satisfaction. "Except for this." She opened a bag and took out a toy dog with long, floppy ears, wrinkled brow and a mournful look. "Here, Karrie," she said. "This is for you."

Karin took the toy and hugged it to her chest. "Thanks, Skye."

"You're welcome." Skye smiled as she kneeled and held out her arms. "Do I get a hug?"

"Two!" Karin said, wrapping her arms around Skye's neck and squeezing twice.

Skye laughed and stood up. "What are you going to call him?"

"Umm—I know. Bags!"

"Bags," Bjorn repeated. "Why?"

"'Cause he's got a baggy face," Karin explained, looking seriously at her father.

Bjorn chucked her under the chin and grinned. "So he does. Good name, kiddo. Now get into bed."

Bjorn waited until Skye had tucked Karin in, then asked if he could talk to her alone. They went into the living room.

"Skye, I meant to give you this earlier." He handed her a folded piece of paper.

Skye looked at it. It was a check made out to her for an amount that made eyes widen.

"I know you've had to neglect your painting lately," he said, "and haven't had a chance to sell much. Consider it wages for taking care of Karin."

Skye thrust the check back at him. "No, Bjorn— thank you, but I won't take it."

"Why not?" He frowned, refusing to take it back. "You've certainly earned it."

"I've never considered taking care of Karin a job," she said quietly. "Please take it back. I don't want it— and to be honest, I don't need it. I—I have money. Quite a lot, actually. My father left it to me." Quickly, she tucked the check into his shirt pocket.

"Are you sure, Skye?"

"Quite sure," she said with a touch of haughtiness. "And even if I didn't have money, I wouldn't want to be paid for... for loving Karin."

Bjorn looked at her, nodding thoughtfully. "In that case," he said, "all I can say is thank you, Skye."

Skye merely nodded and turned away. That wasn't what she wanted from him, either.

For some reason Skye had the impression that Bjorn didn't really like the idea of her having money, and this was confirmed the next day when he took her to a car dealership to look for a new van. To his concern, she bought the first one she saw.

"You know, you might get a better deal elsewhere," he said with a frown.

Skye shrugged. "I'd planned on paying about this much," she explained, "and, anyway, I don't feel like looking all around the city—I've got a hair appointment this afternoon. Besides," she added impishly, "I like the color."

His frown deepened when she casually wrote out a check for the whole amount, but she saw no reason to pretend any longer she was the poor struggling artist he seemed to prefer, whatever his reasons might be. She had money and he would have to accept the fact.

They drove back to the Rosens' separately, Skye enjoying the feel of her new van. They arrived just in time for her to leave with Miri for the hairdresser's.

They returned a few hours later and Skye was pleased that her new haircut met with Bjorn's wholehearted approval. He stared at her for a moment, and then a slow, easy smile spread across his face and he nodded.

"It looks great," he said, touching the soft, shoulder-length curls. "Beautiful, in fact. Like a fine, fluffy cloud."

Skye blushed under his scrutiny. "Thank you, Bjorn," she said shyly. She gave her head a little shake and grinned. "It certainly feels better."

"Bjorn," Miri said, coming into the room, "Dave and I are going to take the kids out for a quick bite to eat. Don't worry—you're spared. You and Skye can relax by the pool and have a nice, peaceful drink."

"Thanks, Miri." Bjorn laughed. "That's the best offer I've had all day."

"Did Miri tell you where we're going tonight?" he asked Skye as they settled into lawn chairs beside the pool.

"Not really. She said something about a boat when we were shopping, but didn't elaborate. She spotted the perfect pair of shoes just as she was about to tell me." Skye kicked off her sandals and wiggled her toes. "Where exactly are we going?"

"On board the *Lord Selkirk*. It used to do weekend excursions on Lake Winnipeg," Bjorn explained. "It underwent some renovations a few years ago and is now used for dinner and dance cruises along the Red River."

"That sounds like fun," Skye said. She left her chair to sit on the side of the pool, dangling her feet in the water. She glanced at Bjorn over her shoulder. "I'm looking forward to it. It's been a long time since I've done any thing like that."

Before Reid, she thought, turning back to the pool, remembering with a ghost of a smile her few dates in university before Reid had begun his courting. She had been so flattered by the older man's attention, his sophisticated wooing, that it wasn't until much later that she'd realized they had never had any fun together—had never done anything spontaneous or exciting. Reid went only where he was sure of being seen by the right people with the right political connections.

Nor, she reflected, staring into the blue-green water, had there ever been any private time between them. His kisses had been perfunctory, without insistence. Skye knew that if she'd been even a little more experienced, she would have known there was something odd about his lack of passion. As it was, she had thought it was very romantic when he told her he wanted to wait until their wedding night to consummate their love. Skye shook her head with rueful amazement. Had that naive and trusting girl really been her?

"Hey, you two—we're back!"

Miri's voice startled her back to awareness. She looked over her shoulder to find Bjorn watching her closely and frowning thoughtfully. She gave him a quick, slightly puzzled smile as Miri came through the patio doors.

"Well, that's done." Miri grinned. "The kids have had their fill of hamburgers and we stopped for ice cream on the way back. Now we can go out with a clear conscience and enjoy!"

SKYE EXAMINED HERSELF critically in the mirror before she went downstairs to join the others. Regular hours of sleep had erased the shadows from under her eyes and plenty of Mary's good cooking had softened her thinness. Her new, flattering haircut framed her tanned face beautifully, accentuating her shining eyes, the dusky curls dancing about her shoulders in a carefree style. She looked better than she had in years.

She chose a yellow cotton dress with a splash of blue design around the hem and a matching casual blue shirt-style jacket with rolled sleeves. The outfit was bright and summery and, when the jacket was removed to reveal her smooth shoulders rising from the strapless top, decidedly sexy. Perfect, Miri had told her, for the evening ahead. After strapping on delicate, high-heeled sandals she left the room, taking a deep, steadying breath.

When she entered the living room Bjorn was sitting with Dave, drink in hand. Bjorn's eyes were fixed on her as he got to his feet and came toward her.

"You look beautiful, Skye," he said, his voice low and intimate. "Absolutely beautiful." He touched a lock of hair where it fell on the jacket.

Skye's lashes swept down in a mixture of pleasure and embarrassment. "Thank you, Bjorn." It was the reaction she had been hoping for. She looked up shyly and met his eyes, happy with the warm admiration she saw reflected there.

"Can I get you a drink, Skye?" Dave asked from across the room.

"No, thank you, Dave," she answered, tearing her eyes from Bjorn's and smiling at Dave. She liked the quiet, friendly man with his observant hazel eyes. "Where's Karin?" she asked, wanting to say good-night before they left.

"In the family room with Rebecca and Jeremy," Dave replied. "I got them a couple of movies for the VCR. Oh, and Rebecca was wondering what time she should put Karin to bed."

Skye and Bjorn headed to the family room and found Karin curled up beside Rebecca on a couch, watching an adventure movie on a large television screen. Jeremy was lying on the floor. Karin looked up and smiled shyly at her father and Skye. "You look pretty," she said to Skye.

"You sure do," Rebecca echoed with her wide grin. "Hey, Bjorn—what time does Karin go to bed?"

"Usually eight-thirty," Bjorn told her. "But tonight I'll leave it up to you."

"Great—I think she'll like the next movie, but if she gets sleepy, I'll put her to bed. Okay?"

"That sounds good to me. And thanks, Rebecca, for baby-sitting."

"That's okay. I have to do it for my ratty brother, anyway." She grinned, jerking a thumb toward Jeremy who promptly stuck out his tongue.

Skye laughed, enjoying their good-natured teasing. "Come give a kiss, Karin," she said, holding out her arms to the girl. "Be a good girl for Rebecca. I'll see you in the morning."

"'Kay," Karin said, snuggling close for a moment. "It's a good show," she confided in her whispery voice.

"I'm glad you're enjoying it." She kissed Karin's cheek. "Say good-night to your dad now."

She went shyly to Bjorn, accepting his kiss with a duck of her head. Not a rejection by any means, Skye noted, but she still hadn't accepted him completely.

"Have fun, kids," Bjorn said, stroking Karin's curls. "Bye, now."

"Bye, Bjorn." They then turned to Skye and chorused, "Bye, Skye," and giggled at the rhyme.

Skye looked at Bjorn and they shared a smile. As they left the room he took her hand, lacing his fingers in hers. She felt a glow of pleasure and her heart beat a little faster in anticipation of the evening ahead.

THE BLUE-AND-WHITE SHIP waited in the wide green-brown waters of the Red River. Dining aboard a ship—especially the *Lord Selkirk*—was quite a novelty for Skye. The food was excellent, the wine mellow. Dave and Miri were wonderful company, and Skye admitted to herself that she and Bjorn were on an actual date, a couple.

"The boat goes back to the dock after dinner," Miri explained, "and then goes out again for the dance cruise. The crowd changes then—it's usually a lot of fun."

Skye smiled and nodded, thinking dreamily about what lay ahead. She couldn't wait to be dancing with Bjorn, she thought with a quiver of excitement. It would be lovely to be held in his arms, if only for a turn or two around the dance floor.

They finished eating and relaxed over coffee and liqueur, watching through the picture window as the tree-lined river banks slipped by, the city an occasional flicker in the background. They watched the sun set, coloring the sky a deep red gold that paled to peach as night came in an indigo rush. Stars shone dim above the haze of city lights and the air was soft and warm. The ship docked and many of the diners left, replaced by an energetic crowd looking forward to an evening of dancing.

"Come on, Dave," Miri said, snapping her fingers and moving her shoulders to the calypso beat of the band. "You promised me you would dance tonight."

"Aw, Miri," he protested. "This isn't my kind of music."

"Well, it's highly unlikely that the Stones are going to drop in," Miri said, taking his hand and tugging. "You'll like it just fine once you get those feet moving. Come on."

"Yes, ma'am," Dave said with an air of resignation, allowing himself to be led to the dance floor.

Skye looked at Bjorn, her eyes twinkling. "Do you need to be coerced, or are you willing?"

"Ready, willing and able," he answered, his eyes fixed on hers. "I'm just waiting for you." Skye thought she caught an undertone to his words, but the blank expression on his relaxed and smiling face gave nothing away.

"Just let me take this off," she said, removing her jacket. Her bare, tanned shoulders gleamed softly in the low light.

Bjorn stood up and took her hand, squeezing her fingers gently as he pulled her to her feet. He ran one finger from her jaw, down her neck and over her shoulder, cupping it in his hand as his eyes held hers.

Skye shivered and felt her breasts tighten. Timidly her lashes swept down to cover her eyes.

"When I first met you," he said, his voice low and intimate, "I thought you were pretty, in a girlish sort of way. Tonight you're a beautiful woman, with an enticing hint of Gypsy about you." He curled a finger under her chin and raised her head until she looked at him, his eyes looking into hers with an intensity that brought color to her cheeks. Smiling, he stepped back, taking her hand. "Let's dance," he said softly.

As Skye molded to the rhythm of his expert steps, desire flowed through her body. She was aware of nothing, no one but Bjorn. Every touch of his hand, every caress told her he saw her as a woman; every heavy-lidded, lingering look told her he desired her. She was flushed and sparkling with excitement, hardly daring to believe what she read in his eyes.

"No need to ask if you're enjoying yourself," Miri grinned later as they went to the ladies' room. Impulsively she squeezed Skye's fingers. "I think you two are made for each other."

The men were at the table when they returned. "Let's go out for some fresh air," Bjorn suggested.

"You two go ahead," Miri insisted, "I'd like to sip my drink for a while." She winked at Skye.

"Okay," Skye said, smiling when Bjorn took her hand in his, leading her out onto the deck.

There were groups of people clustered around, but they managed to find a quiet corner. Leaning against the railing, they watched the rippling glint of water roll away from the ship's passage.

"You have the most beautiful shoulders," Bjorn murmured, running his fingers gently from her earlobe over the curve of her neck and shoulder. "So smooth and satiny. Honeyed." His lips pressed against the back of her neck and she shivered, relaxing against him, her head grazing his cheek. His hands tightened on her arms and he turned her toward him. She could see the desire gleam in his eyes as his mouth covered hers with a sense of urgency.

He had kissed her in sympathy, and he had kissed her with gratitude. But this was a kiss filled with passion and desire and she responded with every fibre of her being. Her lips parted to the delicious thrust of his tongue, her knees weakening and she clung to his shoulders, pushing closer.

His lips left hers suddenly and he buried his face in her hair, holding her tight as he let out his breath. Drawing back, he looked at her, his eyes narrow and dark. He kissed her again, lightly this time, his thumbs caressing her shoulders, and then smiled a little ruefully.

"I'm afraid we might attract an audience," he murmured. He dropped another kiss on her throbbing lips. "Let's go back inside." Holding hands, they went to rejoin Dave and Miri.

When the ship docked, they followed the flow of people to the parking lot. Bjorn sat behind the wheel of Dave's car while Dave and Miri got into the back.

"Bjorn volunteered to drive," Dave explained. "He figures I'll fall off the white line."

"Chances are good," Miri said with an affectionate smile. "But that's okay—we can pretend we're teenagers and neck!"

"Mmm!" Dave said enthusiastically. "I haven't made out in the back seat of a car for—let's see . . . It must have been in 1968 with—"

"Shut up and pucker up," Miri said, jabbing him in the ribs with her elbow. "I'm not interested in your sleazy past."

Skye smiled at their jesting banter and impulsively joined the game by sliding across the front seat, brushing against Bjorn. He smiled at her, taking her hand and raising it to his lips, pressing a warm kiss on the soft skin of her inner wrist.

"Maybe I should have let Dave drive," he murmured, with a quick warm smile. He turned his attention back to the road, but kept her hand, his fingers laced with hers.

The drive, with Bjorn so close and she, filled with dreamy hopes, seemed too short as all too soon they were pulling up in the Rosens' driveway. Dave and Miri walked hand in hand into the house lit only by a dim light in the living room. Skye watched them wistfully in spite of Bjorn's attentiveness. It was obvious that they cared deeply for each other. How wonderful it must be to feel so in love after years of marriage, to know that it's for keeps, that your husband is a cherished friend, a trusted lover....

"Anyone for a nightcap?" Dave asked as they entered the living room.

"Not for me," Bjorn answered.

"Nor me," Skye said. It was obvious to her that Dave and Miri wanted to be alone and she couldn't blame them. It was exactly what she wanted with Bjorn. She glanced at him with a hint of longing but looked away again before his eyes could meet hers. "I think I'll go to bed," she said, her voice low. "Good night, everyone." She bade, then reluctantly, left the room.

It wasn't what she wanted to do, but she had no other choice. She had spent a wonderful, romantic evening with Bjorn, but it had come to an end. There was nothing left but to go to bed, by herself, in a room she shared with his daughter.

Skye crept quietly into the room, feeling her way in the dark to the small lamp on the night table between the two beds and turned it on. Karin was sleeping peacefully, her new toy dog tucked under one arm. Skye sat on the edge of her bed, looking at Karin with a gentle smile. She loved the little girl as her own, and she loved Bjorn, loved the big, gentle man, deeply, fully....

She sighed and bent to unbuckle her shoes. What was loving him going to hold for her? He was a kind and caring man who would never knowingly hurt her; she was sure of that. And after tonight, with all his lingering looks and kisses, she was beginning to hope that maybe, just maybe, he was starting to care for her in return. She felt a glow of excitement and jumped up to prowl about the room. Was he falling in love with her?

The room was too small to contain her sudden restless excitement and she knew sleep was a long way off. Snapping out the light, she tiptoed out of the bedroom, her bare feet making no noise in the carpeted hallway.

The night air was still and warm, a crescent moon casting faint light over the pool. There was a sweet, pervasive scent of honeysuckle from the hedge between the neighboring yards, and she breathed deeply.

Walking around the pool and out onto the end of the diving board, she tested its springiness for a moment before sitting down, the tips of her toes brushing the water. She moved them back and forth, staring dreamily into the trail of moonlight rippling across the pool.

She wasn't really surprised when she looked up and saw Bjorn, in his bathing suit, standing at the opposite end of the pool. As she watched, he walked into the water until it was waist deep. Slowly he lowered himself, stretching out to lazily stroke the surface, his eyes never leaving the place where she sat. Skye's lips parted and her breath became faster as he moved slowly closer.

He treaded water under the diving board for a moment and then grasped her ankles, looking up at her. Skye placed her hands on the edge of the board and leaned forward, smiling down at him.

"Coming in?" he asked, his voice low.

"Uh-uh. I'm not wearing a bathing suit."

One wet hand moved slowly up over her calf and rested on the soft inner skin of her thigh. "I don't mind."

Skye's heart quickened at his touch and she wanted to join him. "Well, in that case . . ." She pulled her legs from his grasp and stood up, casting a quick look at the sleeping house and quiet yard. Her eyes glistening with excitement and daring, she reached around to her back and slowly unzipped her dress, letting it slip over her hips to her ankles. Skye stood for a moment, clad only in lacy panties and a dainty, strapless bra. Stepping out of the dress, she bounced lightly and then arched over Bjorn's head into the water below.

It was cool but refreshing. Skye surfaced and turned, treading water a short distance from Bjorn, laughing at her bravado. With one long, lazy stroke, he was beside her, his teeth glinting in the moonlight as he grinned at her.

"Well, well," he murmured softly, looking closely at her. "You surprised me."

"I surprised myself," Skye admitted with a low laugh, loving the sensuous feel of the water on her skin. "It must have been that last glass of wine." She rolled onto her back, turning her head to smile at him, floating lazily and waiting for his touch.

He swam round behind her, his hands resting on her
shoulders while his legs drifted up under hers. When he
laid his head back in the water, his body arched and
Skye floated against him, her legs loosely entwining
with his. He stroked his arms through the water, pulling them toward the shallow end. When his feet could
touch bottom, he stood up, turning her in his arms.

Smiling, she wrapped her arms around his neck. "I
can't touch bottom," she whispered.

"That's all right," he said huskily. "I wasn't planning on letting go."

"Good." She was floating against him in the cool
water, her body heating where it touched his. She
gripped his legs with hers and pressed closer, her body
overflowing with desire.

His eyes were hooded as he lowered his head to touch
his mouth to hers. His lips felt soft and warm, his body
hard and unyielding against her pliancy. His kiss was
slow and sensuous and she could taste the lingering fla-
vor of wine on his tongue, feel the growing heat of her
body in the cool, moon-sparked water.

His fingers skimmed the swell of her breasts above
the lacy edge of her bra. He felt her breath catch against
his lips and the kiss deepened, became more demanding as his fingers caressed around to her back, fum-
bling for the fastening.

Skye pushed back a bit. "It's a front clasp," she
whispered. Her arms dropped from his neck and she
allowed herself to drift back so that her upper body
floated on the surface of the water, her legs anchoring
her to him. Slowly she undid the bra and then lay still,
feeling the water cooly lap her taut nipples, and then
Bjorn's heated touch as he brushed them with the palms
of his hands. Slowly he drew her closer and then raised

her so their mouths met again and her breasts quivered against the velvet hardness of his chest. She was lost to desire, wanting him, loving him.

"Skye," he murmured against her lips.

"Hmm?"

"It feels wonderful holding you like this," he said, his lips sweeping softly over hers. He cupped her hips and pulled her tight against the impudent hardness of his. "I want you, Skye," he breathed.

Skye moaned softly and buried her head in the heat of his shoulder. Her body clamored to match his passion but her emotions shied nervously from the onslaught of such intense physical need. It was all happening too fast.

"Bjorn," she whispered, "I don't...I'm not quite ready for all this." She raised her head and looked at him, her eyes wide with distress.

Bjorn examined her face closely, then closed his eyes and nodded with a harsh sigh. "It's all right," he said. "I understand." He gave her a short, hard kiss before thrusting himself away from her to swim the length of the pool with strong, rapid strokes.

Wishing fervently that she had been able to let herself be carried away by their passion, Skye retrieved her bra and put it back on. Swimming slowly to the side of the pool, she hauled herself out to sit on the edge and watched Bjorn. She tensed when he swam toward her, hugging her arms against her chest.

He stopped beside her and looked up, moonlight glistening on his face. His hands cupped the backs of her legs and his chest rested against her knees. "Are you okay?" he asked.

"No," she admitted, shivering with a sudden chill. "Bjorn, are you...are you angry with me?"

He pulled himself out of the pool and sat beside her. "Of course not," he said, his voice still thick with suppressed passion. He put his arm around her and held her to his side. "A bit frustrated, I admit," he said with a smile. "But angry—no. Really, Skye, I do understand."

Skye leaned against him with a sigh.

Just being close to him helped diminish the ache, but she was afraid it wouldn't be long before they turned to each other in passion again. But that wouldn't be fair to him, or to herself, for that matter. Skye panicked. Suddenly she pushed away from him and scrambled up, going to find her dress. She pulled it over her wet skin and zipped it up. When she turned, Bjorn was standing in front of her.

They looked at each other for a long moment. Skye touched the side of his face with soft fingers and smiled. She loved him. That was certain. But she wasn't ready for love. "Good night, Bjorn," she whispered.

Bjorn leaned his head down, keeping a chaste distance between their bodies. His lips covered hers in a brief, restrained kiss and then he stepped back. "Good night," he said, his voice low. He dived back into the water as Skye walked slowly, reluctantly, toward the house.

SKYE AWOKE LATE. She grinned and stretched luxuriously, surprised that she had managed to sleep so well. A quick glance at the other bed showed her that Karin was already up, her pink pajamas in a little pile on the floor. The curtains waved in the breeze revealing sunshine and a blue sky. She could hear the deep rumble of Dave's and Bjorn's voices over the chatter of the children.

She felt wonderful. The night before might have had its frustrations, but she now knew just how much Bjorn wanted her. Throwing back the covers, she got out of bed, a smile playing on her lips. What lay ahead? They were already friends, were close to becoming lovers. His attraction to her had to go beyond the physical. Could he be falling in love with her? Remembering how patient and understanding he had been, Skye felt a growing confidence that just maybe he was.

Lifting the corner of the curtain, she looked outside. Karin sat at the far end of the pool near the kitchen, eating cereal with Rebecca and Jeremy. Dave and Bjorn were leaning back in lawn chairs, sipping from mugs of steaming coffee. Their deep voices carried easily to Skye.

"Any last-minute advice, Dave?" Bjorn asked, inclining his head toward Karin.

Dave was looking into his coffee, swirling it gently. "I can't think of anything," he said thoughtfully. "Just be patient. And—"

"And?" Bjorn prompted.

"Well," Dave said, rubbing his chin, "I've been watching her with Skye. There's a pretty strong bond between the two of them, Bjorn. It's going to be rough on Karin when Skye leaves."

"Yeah," Bjorn said, frowning. "I've been thinking about that."

"Any chance of her staying on? At least until your relationship with Karin is stronger."

Bjorn ran a finger around the rim of his mug. "At first I thought I could just hire her to stay for a few months," he said. "But she set me straight about that. Money isn't going to do it."

"So?"

Bjorn shrugged. "So—maybe I'll marry her."

Dave's eyebrows arched in surprise. "What? You? The confirmed—reconfirmed bachelor?"

"But that's just it. I'm not really a bachelor anymore, am I? I'm a single father with a daughter who needs a mother. Skye is almost one to her already."

Dave nodded. "That's true, but the question is, would the lady be willing?"

"Oh, I think she might be persuaded," Bjorn drawled. "She's very fond of Karin. I doubt that she's anxious to leave her. That's a point in my favor," he added, as though weighing the possibilities. "And last night I assured myself she's not immune to my, ah...charms." Skye was sure she detected a certain smugness in his voice and she felt a queasiness in the pit of her stomach. "If everything goes the way I want it, I'd say I can have her where I want her within a couple of months."

Dave shook his head slowly and grinned. "You sound pretty darn sure of yourself, old buddy. And I must admit, it could be ideal for Karin. But do—"

Skye had heard more than enough. She let the curtain fall and backed away from the window, feeling sick. Dropping heavily to her bed, she held her clenched hands tight to her stomach. How *could* he?

She had heard echoes of Reid's voice behind Bjorn's calculating words. The sharp and unpleasant memories of the time, shortly after their wedding, when it had become blatantly obvious that he didn't love her, surfaced in her mind. She remembered summoning up enough courage to confront her husband.

"Why did you marry me?" she'd asked in a pained whisper, pulling the sheet up over her body, as he exited her bedroom.

Reid turned back from the doorway. There was a hint of contempt in his cold eyes as they swept over her. "I needed a wife," he said expressionlessly. "You were... convenient."

Convenient. That was really what Bjorn had been saying to Dave. He would find it convenient to marry her, for Karin's sake. Had she been so foolish as to fall in love, again, with a man who was pretending interest just to use her? Her eyes closed against a rush of pain. Is that all last night had been—a pretense?

Her eyes flew open and she looked about the room with a feeling of panic. Jumping up, she grabbed her robe and headed for the bathroom across the hall. Leaning against the door for a moment, she fought back a sick, sinking feeling and then flung the shower curtain aside, turning on the hot water. By the time she got out, she felt more in control and went back to her room to dress.

It had hurt badly to overhear Bjorn contemplating marriage to her in order to provide Karin with security. It had hurt to realize that his kisses and caresses hadn't been based on honest feelings, but had been part of his plan. *Plan.* Angrily she tugged a comb through her hair. Why couldn't he have just admitted to her that he felt worried about how Karin would handle her leaving? He had to know how much she cared for the child. If he'd wanted her to stay, why didn't he just ask?

Skye tossed down the comb and prowled agitatedly about the room, struggling to prepare herself to face Bjorn. From now on, she would be polite but distant. What had happened the night before wouldn't go any further. She would let him think she had been momentarily carried away, perhaps by too much to drink. As soon as they got back to his place, she would make arrangements to leave. Taking a deep breath, she tightened her lips determinedly. She would not be used again.

Miri had joined the men by the pool and was clutching a mug of coffee and blinking sleepily.

"Here she is," Dave said cheerfully, rising from his chair. "Just in time, Skye. I'm about to make my famous Sunday omelet."

Skye's lips moved in a stiff smile. "Don't make any for me," she said. "I'm not hungry. I—I must have had a bit too much to drink last night," she added with a grimace, giving Bjorn a quick, cool look before turning back to Dave. "Really—I couldn't eat a thing."

"I don't have much of an appetite, either," Miri said, smothering a yawn. "You're getting off light today, Davey-boy."

Skye sat on the chair Dave had vacated, studiously avoiding Bjorn's eyes. She knew he was watching her closely, but she wasn't strong enough to meet his eyes and pretend nothing had happened. Not yet. She needed more time to distance herself. Nervously she rubbed the palms of her hands together, hoping she would be able to find the strength she needed to get through the next few days.

"Hangover?" Miri murmured, taking in Skye's still features.

"A bit." Skye managed to smile. "Wine does that to me if I'm not careful. And last night, I wasn't careful," she added with a tinge of bitterness she couldn't conceal. She leaned back in her chair and closed her eyes. She'd let them think she wasn't feeling well because she'd had too much to drink. She'd let Bjorn think she had responded to him for no reason other than the effects of the wine.

She was aware that he was watching her, a puzzled frown cutting his brow. When he talked to her, she managed to keep her responses cool and impersonal. He made a couple of attempts to talk to her alone, but she found it was easy to avoid him in the bustle of getting ready to leave. When they were back at his place Skye knew it would be impossible, and she prayed that she'd be able to maintain her aloofness when he did manage to get her alone.

She loved him and she wanted him and, in spite of what she had overheard, wondered if she would be able to resist him.

CHAPTER SEVEN

THE TRIP BACK seemed endless. Skye easily adjusted to driving the new van and followed at a safe distance behind Bjorn and Karin, struggling to keep her mind on her driving.

Everything had seemed so simple the night before. Excited by the new feelings Bjorn had aroused in her, she had been looking forward to the future, hopeful of having an honest relationship with a decent, caring man. And now... She clenched the steering wheel tightly and stared at the straight, stretching highway. The truth cut deeply.

She played the words she'd overheard Bjorn speak to Dave again and again in her mind hoping to find another meaning, but the message was all too clear. He had once said that he would do anything for Karin. It hadn't occurred to her that would mean contemplating marriage solely for the child's sake. It hurt unbearably to realize that there had been nothing real about the romance and passion in the pool. He had been manipulating her feelings, testing her response to him, wondering if there was enough of an attraction to create a satisfactory physical relationship between them.

Well, it's not going any further, Skye thought grimly, remembering with a wince the smugness in his voice while he talked to Dave. As soon as she returned, she would make plans to leave. One man had married her because she was convenient and useful to him. She would not let it happen again.

She was relieved when they finally turned onto the gravel driveway leading to the house. She parked her van beside his car and got out stiffly, going around to the side door for her suitcase.

"Let me get that," Bjorn said, coming up behind her.

"I can manage, thanks," Skye said, pleased with the cool distance in her voice.

Bjorn was frowning. "Skye, what's wrong?"

Before she could form an answer, Mary came out of the house. "Skye," she called. "You've got a visitor." A man stepped out behind her.

Skye's eyes widened with surprise and a smile of delight lit her face. "Theo!" Dropping her suitcase, she ran toward him and was enveloped in a warm bear hug against a strong, barrel chest. "Theo!" she exclaimed again, pushing back to look at him. "When did you get here?"

Theo grinned and gave her a hearty buss on each cheek, his bushy beard tickling her with comforting familiarity. "Just this morning," he said, examining her face closely. "How are you, kid?"

Skye shrugged, her face clouding again. "All right— considering."

"We'll talk later," he said as Bjorn came up to them, his face dark and frowning. Theo kept one arm around her as she made introductions.

"Bjorn," she said, her voice level, "this is Theo Brenner. A very good friend of mine," she added. "Theo—Bjorn Stefansson."

She watched as the two men shook hands, Theo with his usual heartiness, Bjorn stiffly, his eyes narrowed and studying her friend closely. "And this is Karin," she said, drawing the girl closer. "Karin, this is my friend, Theo."

Theo hunkered down, his arms resting on his thighs. "Hello, Karin," he said, his brown eyes gentle. "Skye told me a lot about you in her letters—especially how you like to play with Bess."

Karin ducked her head shyly, peeping sideways at Theo. "She likes to chase sticks," she whispered.

Theo grinned. "She sure does. Skye and I used to throw sticks for her on the beach in Vancouver. Maybe we can all go down to the lake later and throw some for her." He smiled at Karin again and then straightened, looking at Bjorn. "Hope you don't mind me staying tonight, Bjorn," he said. "Mary was kind enough to let me pitch my tent down by the lake."

"Any friend of Skye's is welcome here," Bjorn said politely. "In fact, you're welcome to stay in the house with us."

Theo shook his head. "Thanks, but I'm comfortable where I am. I'm on my way east," he explained. "Thought I'd spend a week or two in Quebec City, maybe head down to the Gaspé for a bit."

"A painting holiday?" Skye asked, still comfortable in the circle of his arm.

"Yeah. I wanted a change of scenery."

"You're an artist, too." Bjorn stated.

"I am," Theo said. "But not as good as this one's going to be," he added, squeezing Skye's shoulder affectionately.

Skye smiled. "Theo also works with disturbed children as an art therapist," she volunteered, very aware of Bjorn's narrow-eyed scrutiny as he watched the two of them. Bjorn's suspiciousness pleased her. If Bjorn thought that Theo was more to her than a good friend, he might leave her alone. With Theo's natural, open-hearted affection, it shouldn't be too hard to convince him that something was going on between them. It might make things easier for her, save the pride that a direct confrontation would destroy. She squeezed Theo's arm and smiled at him. Theo wouldn't mind. He would come through for her.

"Well," Mary said, breaking the silence and looking thoughtfully at the three of them, "Theo and I were just about to sit down with a pitcher of iced tea. Why don't we all go to the back patio? You must be thirsty after that long drive."

At Mary's insistence, Theo stayed for supper as well. He was jovial and friendly, gently teasing Karin and charming Mary by enthusiastically praising her cooking.

"I hope you've been giving Skye lessons." He grinned with a broad wink. "That woman is hopeless in the kitchen. She'd rather paint food than cook it."

Skye pulled a face at him as she pinched his cheek playfully. "And you would rather eat it. You, Theo my friend, are doomed to be . . . portly."

Theo pushed back his chair and patted his stomach. "True," he chuckled. "Undoubtedly true."

Skye got up and began clearing the table, darting quick glances at Bjorn. His face looked cold and hard again, the animation gone from his eyes. But Skye didn't feel sympathy for him anymore. He had sounded so sure of himself when he had outlined his plans to Dave, thinking she would be easily persuaded. He hadn't counted on Theo, and Skye had been subtly implying all afternoon that Theo was more than a friend. Theo caught on quickly and had played along, but she could see the questions dancing in her friend's brown eyes.

Over Mary's protests, Theo helped to clear the table before making his excuses to leave. "That was a wonderful meal. Thank you, Mary—Bjorn. You too, squirt." He grinned at Karin, affectionately ruffling her hair. "Come on, bright eyes," he said to Skye, holding out his hand. "You can walk me to the tent."

Smiling, Skye put her hand in his, allowing him to pull her to her feet. "Good night, Karin," she said, dropping Theo's hand to hug the little girl. "I'll see you in the morning."

"Aren't you going to tuck me in?" she asked.

"Not tonight, sweetheart. Your daddy will."

"Oh." There was a note of doubt in her voice as she stole a look at her father.

"I'll even read you your favorite story." Bjorn's voice was gentle as he spoke to his daughter, but Skye caught the set look of his face.

She gave Karin a fast kiss and stood up, turning to Theo and taking his hand again. "Don't wait up," she called over her shoulder, seeing Bjorn's face darken as they left, followed closely by the dog.

"Okay, Skye Cameron. What's up?" Theo asked as soon as they were out of earshot.

Skye's shoulders slumped and she sighed wearily. "Nothing much. Just my usual emotional mess."

"Things aren't going so well between you and your Viking, I take it." Theo had remembered that she'd called him a Viking in one of her letters. "I've seen warmer looks on a marble statue."

"He's not my Viking," Skye started. "At least—"

"Wait until we get to my camp," Theo interrupted. "I've got a bottle of wine in the cooler. We can sit around a fire and quietly get smashed while you tell Uncle Theo all about it.''

Skye smiled mistily and nodded, thinking about how much she owed to Theo's friendship.

He had pulled his old, dusty blue car under a gnarled and twisted peachleaf willow. His bright red two-man tent was pitched beside it on the grassy ground. Flat stones had been stacked into a circular fire pit and a pile of fallen branches awaited the match.

Skye sat down and leaned against a wooden box Theo used as a table, watching him move about in the lingering twilight, lighting the fire and opening the wine. Bess lay by her side. She smiled her thanks when Theo handed her a Styrofoam cup filled with wine. He added more wood to the fire and sat beside her.

Skye took a sip of her wine and grimaced. ''Styrofoam does not enhance cheap wine.''

Theo grinned. ''I'm roughing it. Besides, it smooths out a lot after the first glass or two.'' His voice became gentler and he looked at her, the flames dancing in his brown eyes. ''I'm all ears, hon,'' he said.

''All heart is more like it,'' Skye said, giving him a rather weak smile. ''Are you sure you want to hear it this time?''

''If it'll help you to talk about it, then of course I want to listen.'' He put an arm around her shoulders and gave her a quick squeeze. ''Last letter I got from you, you sounded on top of it all. What happened?''

Skye's lips twisted in a self-mocking smile. ''I fell in love with the wrong man. Again. Nothing new.''

''Stefansson, I take it.''

She nodded, staring at the flames dancing bright against the darkening sky.

"When you say the wrong man again, does that mean you're comparing him to Reid?" Theo frowned. "I'll admit he seemed a bit well, grim, but I would have thought he was an okay kind of guy."

Skye took a sip of wine. "No," she said slowly. "I'm not comparing him to Reid." In all honesty, she couldn't. Tonelessly she told Theo what had happened.

"I guess I understand, in a way," she continued. "He's carrying around a lot of guilt over Karin. I know he's just trying to make things up to her. But," she added with a bitter sadness, "why couldn't he be honest? In that way, I have to compare him to Reid. They both pretended something they didn't feel in order to get what they wanted from me, regardless of my feelings."

"Ah, kid, that's tough," Theo sympathized, tightening his arm on her shoulders. "Are you sure about it, though?"

"Yeah, I'm sure." She sighed wearily. "I noticed that he didn't seem to like it when I refused his check, that I wasn't poor and struggling as he'd first thought I was. So his offer to pay me to stay with Karin wouldn't work. It was right after he found out that the . . . the romancing began. It's all clear now." She downed her wine and held out the cup. "Could I have some more, please, Theo."

He filled her cup, topping off his own. "What are you going to do now?"

Skye shrugged. "Leave. I'll stay another day or two. I have to let Karin know, give her time to get used to the idea."

"Why don't you talk to him, Skye? Tell him what you heard."

"No!" Skye shook her head emphatically. "I can't. I want to leave with a bit of pride this time," she added bitterly.

"Where will you go?"

"Back to Vancouver." Skye sipped her wine. "Can I stay at your place until I find somewhere of my own?"

"Hey—anytime. You know that. I'd ask you to join me in Quebec, but, ah, there's this woman I met in the spring, and..."

"Uh-oh. Is it romance this time or another one of your lame ducks?"

Theo rolled his eyes and sighed lustily. "Romance. Definitely romance." He put on a French accent. "Her name is Véronique and she's built like a centerfold. Gorgeous creature."

Skye had to laugh. Theo loved women. In the time she had known him, there had been several. Some were lovers, others, like her, friends. "Aren't you ever going to get married?" she asked.

Theo grinned. "Maybe when I'm old and gray—grayer. And too tired for the chase." He yawned suddenly and stretched his arms over his head. "I hate to break this up, kid, but I started off before dawn today. I'm beat."

"Go to bed," she said. "I think I'll stay here for a while and watch the fire."

"Suit yourself." Theo stood up and stretched again. "But if you're just trying to avoid the Viking, I still say you should talk to him."

Skye smiled noncommittally. "Yes, well, good night, Theo." she said.

"Good night, bright eyes." Theo smiled affectionately and went to his tent, stooping to pat the dog on his way. "Hey—I almost forgot. It's your birthday Tuesday and I don't have a present for you."

Skye waved a hand dismissively. "Don't worry about it. I'm not in a birthday mood right now, anyway. I'll let you take me out for dinner when you get back to Vancouver."

"It's a date." Theo yawned and started to unzip the tent flap.

"Theo." Skye looked at him when he turned back to her. "Don't go telling anyone about the birthday, okay? I'd rather no one knew."

Theo smiled and nodded as he knelt to crawl into the tent.

Skye watched him disappear inside and then turned back to the fire, thinking about Theo's advice. What would happen if she went to Bjorn and told him what she'd overheard? Would he be embarrassed and admit to scheming or would he deny everything, pretend that she had misunderstood what he had said? She frowned and dug her thumbnail into the rim of the Styrofoam cup. Either way, facing Bjorn was something she wanted to avoid. What was there to be gained by confronting him? It would be unpleasant and painful and wouldn't change anything, certainly not the way he felt about her. She decided it would be better to just slip quietly away.

She leaned forward and poked a stick into the dying fire, sending a dusting of sparks spiraling upward. When would she leave? If Theo left by noon tomorrow as he'd planned, she could spend the afternoon with Karin and...

Karin. She'd probably suffer the most from her departure. The poor child would be caught in the middle again, not quite ready to love her father, about to lose someone she loved again. Skye blinked back tears and jabbed harder at the coals. It was going to be painful to leave, but she could see no other way.

She waited until the fire had died away to graying embers before she called softly to the dog and left. It was very late, the darkness thick and enveloping. With her hand on the dog's head, she carefully picked her way back to the house.

As she started to open the door to her room, a hand grabbed her wrist, the fingers hard and biting. She jumped back with a short scream of shock.

"What! Bjorn!" She lowered her voice to an indignant whisper. "What do you think you're doing?"

"Waiting," he said succinctly, through clenched teeth. "Do you know what time it is?"

"I haven't a clue. What's more, I don't care." She could see only part of his face in the shadowed darkness, but could feel his fingers on her wrist, tight and unyielding. "Theo and I had a lot to talk about," she added, her voice softening to a purr.

He swore in a muffled voice and pulled her into his arms, his mouth finding hers instantly.

His kiss was hard and plundering, anger underlying passion. For a moment Skye resisted, pushing against his chest to free herself. But passion overcame her as she wrapped her arms around his neck and pressed her body to his, the tip of her tongue stroking his with delicate sensuality.

With a sudden, twisting movement he pushed her away. "Your little...talk seems to have left you wanting," he said harshly.

Skye closed her eyes and sagged against the wall. "What is it you want, Bjorn?" she asked wearily.

"Are you leaving with him?" he demanded.

"I'm very tempted," she said, her voice hardening.

"What about Karin?"

"Yes—what about Karin?" Skye was bitter. "I care for her too much to just walk away without preparing her for it. I will be leaving soon, however, so I suggest, Bjorn Stefansson, that instead of skulking around in dark hallways, you start thinking of some way to endear yourself to your daughter before it's too late. She's your responsibility, not mine!" With that, she flung open her bedroom door and disappeared inside, slamming the door shut behind her, not caring whom she woke up.

She stumbled to her bed and sat down, resting her head in her hands, her stomach churning with anger and cheap wine. Bjorn had been rude and insulting, angry with her because he could see his plans for her going awry.

Bone tired and hurting, she shed her clothes and crawled under the covers. Closing her eyes, she pushed all her troubled thoughts aside, shutting her mind to everything but sleep.

WHEN SHE AWOKE Karin was perched on the edge of the bed, clutching her toy dog under one arm.

"Bags an' me were waiting and waiting for you to wake up," she said.

"Well, I'm awake now." Skye smiled and stretched, pushing herself into a sitting position. "Know what I need today?"

"What?"

"A hug," Skye said, holding out her arms. "A big hug. The best you've got."

Grinning, Karin scampered across the bed and threw herself into Skye's arms, squeezing tight. "There. Was that good?"

"One more time, lovey," Skye whispered against the silken curls.

"Are you sad today?" Karin asked.

"Yes," Skye said honestly. "I am."

Karin leaned back on her heels and looked seriously at her. "How come?"

"Because I'm going to have to leave soon, sweetheart." Skye touched her soft cheek gently.

"You mean...go away from me?" Karin's eyes widened and welled with tears.

"Yes, Karrie," Skye explained, trying to hold back tears. "But your daddy will still be here with you. He loves you a lot, Karin. He won't leave you again."

"Will you come back?"

"I—I can't promise. But if I can come for a visit, I will." That was the best she could do without leaving the child with false hopes.

Karin's bottom lip trembled. "Now I'm sad, too," she cried, burrowing her face in Skye's shoulder. "I wish you could stay."

It was all Skye could do to keep her tears back as she rubbed the child's thin shoulders and murmured comforting words. She looked up and saw Bjorn standing in the doorway, his face set in bleak lines.

"Karin," he said, his voice much more tender than the look on his face. "Mary has your breakfast ready. Come downstairs with me while Skye gets dressed." Karin turned her head from Skye's shoulder and looked at her feather hesitatingly.

"Away you go, sweetie," Skye said with a final hug. "I'll see you in a few minutes."

Karin slid off the bed and went slowly to the door. Bjorn held out his hand and after a moment she put hers into it, looking up at her father, her eyes wide and solemn.

"Skye's right, Karin," he said gruffly. "I love you and I'll never leave you again. I promise." He touched her curls lightly and smiled. "Let's go downstairs now. Mary's waiting."

Skye watched them go, her throat tight with unshed tears, unable to let go of the feeling that she belonged with them. She twisted her mother's wedding ring on her finger, thinking ironically that while it might have served to protect her from an unwanted proposition or two, it had done nothing to protect her from falling in love with the wrong man. Suddenly it seemed senseless to keep wearing it. Slowly she took it off and put it on the bedside table, rubbing the wide, white mark it left on her finger. With a weary sigh, she dashed away the tears that threatened to fall and went to shower.

"Sorry I can't stay for your birthday, Skye," Theo said slyly as he packed his car. "But I've got to get to Quebec by the weekend."

"It's your birthday?" Karin asked, brightening suddenly.

"Tomorrow, actually," Theo answered for Skye, ignoring her warning look.

"Oh, goody!" Karin turned to Bjorn, her eyes wide with excitement. "Can we have a party with balloons an' hats an' stuff? I never had a party," she added wistfully. "I've seen them on TV."

Skye saw Bjorn's eyes darken and knew Karin's comment heightened his anger toward his ex-wife. He put his hands on his daughter's shoulders and gave them a squeeze. "Well, come November, kiddo, you'll have the best party ever," he promised. "In the meantime you can practice by helping Mary make a cake for Skye. If it's all right with Mary, of course," he glanced in her direction.

"Please, Mary, please!" Karin danced with excitement. "I'll help really good an' I'll even remember to wash my hands first. Please!"

Mary's hazel eyes twinkled, and she winked at Skye. "Oh, I guess I can manage to bake one as long as I get lots of help."

Skye wanted to protest, but for Karin's sake kept quiet. The child was excited and happy, looking forward to the party instead of brooding over Skye's departure as she had been all morning. Skye knew the party would be for Karin and not for her, especially as far as Bjorn was concerned. She looked at him and thought, with a pang, that she hadn't seen him smile lately. She missed it, missed the companionship they had begun to share and wished again that she could ignore what she'd overheard.

When Theo's car was packed he said his good-byes, thanking Bjorn and Mary.

"When will you be leaving?" he asked Skye when he others had gone inside.

"Well, my friend, you've made sure it won't be tomorrow. A day or two after that, I suppose. I'll see how it goes with Karin."

"You really love that kid, don't you?" Theo asked gently.

Skye nodded. "Yes, I do."

"And the Viking?"

"In spite of everything—yes," she admitted.

"Then why are you leaving?"

Skye frowned and looked at him. "I told you what he wants from me—how far he's prepared to go to ease his guilt over Karin, the pretense.... What else can I do?" she asked.

"Go to him. Tell him what you heard and ask him to be honest with you. Maybe, just maybe, you misunderstood. Isn't it worth forfeiting just a bit of pride to find out?"

"Pride isn't something I have a lot of, Theo," Skye said bitterly. "Not after Reid. No, I can't go to him. There is no misunderstanding over what I heard. He couldn't buy me so he was going to woo me—falsely. I've been there before. I won't let it happen again."

Theo shook his head. "Skye, you're—"

"It's time you were going, Theo," Skye interrupted. "Kiss me good-bye, will you? And make it look good just in case anyone's watching.

"Yes, ma'am."

Theo's lips were soft, his beard pleasantly ticklish, but there was no spark of desire between them. No matter what it may have seemed to an onlooker, it was a chaste kiss of fond friendship.

"Good luck with what's 'er name," Skye said, breaking away.

"Véronique," Theo said and added pertly. "Luck I don't need. Wish me stamina."

Skye laughed as he got in his car and started the engine. She leaned down and kissed his cheek. "Bye, Theo," she said warmly. "Thanks—again. And drive carefully." She watched as he pulled away.

Theo had been a buffer between her and Bjorn. What would happen now that he had left? Would Bjorn try to carry on with his plans, or had he gotten the message that she was involved with Theo? Skye drew a deep breath and turned back to the house. She hoped Bjorn would leave her alone, be polite and distant, let her get through the next couple of days without added stress and pain.

Bjorn came out on the front steps. "I want to talk to you," he said grimly.

"What about?" Skye said calmly, feeling her stomach clench in apprehension.

"You and Brenner," he said, jerking his chin in the direction of the highway. "What's he to you?"

Skye raised her eyebrows haughtily. "I can't see that it's any of your business, Bjorn."

He grabbed her hand and growled. "After what happened between us in the city, I say it is."

"Nothing happened between us," Skye said, carefully controlling her voice and trying to ignore his tight grip on her fingers. "We shared a few kisses, that's all. Chalk it up to shipboard romance, if you want," she added, forcing a light laugh.

His hand tightened on hers. "Damn it, Skye—" He stopped abruptly and held up her hand. "You're not wearing your ring," he said unexpectedly, staring at her bare finger with the white mark sharp against her tan.

Skye shook her head, puzzled. "No. I decided it was time to take it off."

"I see." Bjorn's voice was flat. He dropped her hand and walked stiffly into the house, letting the screen door slam shut behind him.

Skye rubbed her fingers, staring after him. What was that all about? She sighed and shook her head. It really didn't matter, she told herself. All she wanted was for him to leave her alone.

CHAPTER EIGHT

LUNCH WAS QUIET except for Karin's excited chatter about the shopping trip to Gimli Bjorn had planned for the two of them that afternoon. She was talking openly to her father, her reserve gone. As much as Skye's heart ached, she was happy to see father and daughter drawing closer together. At least she could always look back and know that her stay had accomplished some good.

After they had left, Skye sat with Mary on the back steps, helping her to shell peas for freezing.

"Bjorn says you'll be leaving soon," Mary stated, splitting a pod and dropping the peas into a bowl she held between her knees. "Will you meet up with Theo?"

"No. I'll go back to Vancouver. Theo and I are just friends."

"Oh?" Mary was silent for a moment. "Bjorn and Karin are going to miss you."

"Karin might, for a time," Skye said. "But she'll be happy with her father now."

Mary nodded. "True enough, I suppose. But she needs a mother."

"Bjorn will undoubtedly meet someone soon, now that he's sorted things out with Karin," Skye responded steadily.

"Could be," Mary agreed. "And what would you think about that?"

"I'd wish them all the best," Skye said calmly.

"Could be years before it happens, though," Mary went on stealing glances at Skye's face. "Bjorn's quite shy, you know."

Skye looked at Mary in surprise. "Bjorn—shy? I wouldn't have thought that."

"Oh, yes." Mary nodded decisively. "He's learned to cover it up over the years, but it's still there inside him."

"It sounds as though you've known him for a long time." She had assumed Bjorn had met Mary when he moved from Toronto.

"Most of his life—didn't I say? His grandmother and I were cousins of a sort, though she was years older. Bjorn was always visiting here with his grandparents— he'd always felt he belonged here more than with his own family. They lived just down the road," she added. "The house is gone now, though—torn down a few years ago."

"What was he like as a boy?"

Mary picked up another pod and rubbed it between her fingers until it was a shiny green. "Quiet," she said. "Dreamy. Seemed he'd rather sit and listen to his grandfather's stories than do any of the things boys are supposed to do. His sister was always the more forward of the two." She split the pod with her thumbnail. "He was awful close to his dad. It was a real blow when he died sudden like that—Bjorn was twelve. And then, within six months, his mother decided they'd move down east." She shook her head slowly. "I read some of the letters he wrote to his grandparents—very expressive he was, even then. He became a very lonely and sad little boy."

Mary stopped and straightened her back, rubbing a kink. "But that was a long time ago. He's made good and he's a kind, caring man. There's too few like him in the world.'' She looked closely at Skye. "All I'm saying is that deep down inside, he's sometimes, well, shy and a little bit uncertain.''

Skye said nothing. Shy and uncertain—okay, she got Mary's message and might have believed it if she hadn't overheard Bjorn talking to Dave. He had sounded all too certain then—certain of what he wanted, certain of her response. Mary might think he still possessed some of his little-boy vulnerability, but Skye knew just how wrong she was. Regardless of his motives, he was a conniver and a user. Scowling, Skye split the pod in her hand with a force that sent the peas bouncing down the steps to disappear in the grass.

Just then Karin came running around the side of the house, clutching a plastic shopping bag. "Don't look, Skye," she said breathlessly, holding the bag against her chest. "It's surprises for tomorrow.''

"Let's go find a hiding place," Bjorn said, coming up behind her. "We don't want Skye to cheat and take a peek, do we?'' His words were teasing, but the look he gave Skye was cold.

"No way!" Karin responded with a giggle. "When can we wrap them?''

"After supper, kiddo. I'll help you.''

"'Kay." Karin grinned and jumped back as Skye made a mock grab toward the bag. "Not yet, Skye," she admonished. "Tomorrow! When can we bake the cake, Mary?''

"First thing in the morning," Mary said. "What's your favorite, Skye?''

"Chocolate." Skye was pleased with Karin's glow of excitement. "Definitely chocolate.''

"Then chocolate it is," Mary said, standing up and shaking her apron. "In the meantime, how does fried chicken sound for supper tonight?"

As usual, Mary's dinner had been delicious, though the tension between Bjorn and Skye was thick. After dinner Skye put Karin to bed, kissing her a fond goodnight, then quietly closed the bedroom door. She wanted to avoid Bjorn, not caring how obvious she might be. Stealing cautiously down the stairs, she slipped out the front door.

She walked along the lake with Bess, letting the warm water swirl about her ankles. The lake was calm, the evening almost tranquil. As so often happened, the wind died as the sun began to set. A few clouds stretched long and thin over the horizon and Venus gleamed like a beacon low in the sky. Terns made gliding flights along the shore, heads down and alert for the silvery flash of minnows.

Skye climbed the sandy bank through the willows to the spot where Theo had camped. There was no sign of his presence but the crushed grass where his tent had been and the ashen remains of the fire. She sat down under the peachleaf, leaning against the rough bark, appreciating the solitude.

Bess sat beside her for a while, her wide black muzzle raised to catch the night scents wafting past. Soon her ears pricked, and she was off to chase something, disappearing in the deepening dusk.

Skye closed her eyes and breathed deeply as the air cooled around her, sensing a fraction of the odors that had enticed the dog. A whippoorwill called from the distance as the last of the light disappeared and the heavens glimmered with stars.

She was surprised at how relaxed she felt, how clear her course of action seemed and how she was able to keep the pain at bay. Her years with Reid and the agony of Jennifer's death had left her stronger than she'd realized.

She would leave by the end of the week, she decided. Karin would suffer, but she'd probably be able to turn to her father for comfort. Her leaving should serve to strengthen the tenuous bond between them. What would Bjorn feel when she left? Not too much, Skye had to acknowledge, feeling a stab of pain. Whatever they had shared had been her closeness to Karin. As soon as he realized that his daughter could manage without her, he would breathe a sigh of relief that he had avoided a loveless marriage. Before long, Skye would be a hazy memory for both of them.

Skye sighed and moved her head restlessly against the tree trunk. What about her? She would survive. She had before and she would again, but how much more bitter and distrustful would she be after this?

If only she could feel disgusted with Bjorn, grown to dislike him, but in spite of everything she still couldn't help loving him. If anything, she understood Bjorn's action. If he had been open and honest about what he was feeling, it would have made all the difference to Skye's outlook. What rankled her wasn't so much that he wanted her to stay, perhaps marry her, for Karin's sake, but the way in which he had gone about it. She couldn't help but compare his deceit to Reid's.

True, that was as far as the comparison went. Her mature love for Bjorn couldn't touch the starry-eyed crush she'd had on Reid before their marriage. Bjorn would never abuse her, trample on her dreams and hopes. He would never destroy her love with abject cruelty and disdain. Unlike Reid, he liked and respected her. She had no doubt about that.

But no matter how different the two men were, there was one glaring similarity. Reid had used her to satisfy his needs. Bjorn had contemplated the same, with just as little regard to her feelings.

"Skye?"

For an instant she thought it might be a bird murmuring in the night. Then she heard it again and knew Bjorn was close by. She pressed against the tree, wanting to remain hidden. He called again, closer this time, and she realized the futility of trying to hide. In the star-studded darkness, her white cotton dress would beckon to him.

"Skye, where are you?"

"Here," she said, keeping her voice low, hoping he wouldn't find her.

He came from across the clearing to crouch beside her. "I saw you heading in this direction," he said. "I thought you might be here."

Skye said nothing, wishing she could see more than the shadowy outline of his face.

"You've been avoiding me since the Rosens'," he stated quietly.

"Yes," she said honestly.

"Why? Are you feeling guilty about what happened?"

"Yes," she lied.

Bjorn was silent for a moment. "Are you going to marry him?" he blurted out.

"He hasn't asked me." Her hands clenched nervously. She was acutely aware of his closeness.

"Then why the guilt?" he asked. "You liked what happened. I'm not a fool, Skye. Don't pretend."

"Who's pretending?" she asked lightly. "It was . . . fun." Go away, she thought desperately. Please go away.

"Fun is the wrong word, Skye," he said softly. "It was sensuous, passionate . . . we came very close to making love." He stroked the soft, warm skin from her neck to her shoulders, enticing feelings she longed to keep hidden.

"It would have been good for us, Skye," he whispered huskily. "Damned good." His fingers brushed across the front of her dress and her breath caught audibly. "Fireworks," he breathed with a smile in his voice, running one finger down her breast to stop and lightly stroke the nipple that thrust to meet his touch.

With a quiet moan, Skye turned to him, clasping his head in her hands as her mouth covered his, hot and urgent. He groaned deep in his throat, his arms wrapping around her, pulling her tight against him, straining hard against her fluidity. His tongue thrust deep to be met by hers, as she caressed his inner moistness. She felt the intense passion coursing through her veins and knew she could not deny him anything this time.

His hands found the hem of her dress and skimmed up over her thighs to stroke urgently through the silken barrier. Weak with need, Skye moved against him, clutching, then caressing his shoulders, finding the buttons on his shirt and baring his chest to her touch.

With an abrupt movement, his hands left her and she heard the rustle of hastily discarded clothing. Impatient for his touch on her skin, she undid her dress and drew it over her head. Reaching through the darkness, she touched the satiny swell of his buttocks, moaning softly as he caught her in his arms and pulled her tight to his nakedness, feeling the urgent thrust of his arousal. In the velvet night, there was nothing but his arousing touch, his taste, his scent....

He gently pulled her down on the grass, his mouth on hers, his passion strong and demanding. She answered with her liquid, arching body, her caresses urgent, her breathless murmurs becoming pleas, then whispered cries of fulfillment.

SKYE LAY STILL with Bjorn's arms holding her tight against his chest. She opened her eyes slowly, seeing the soft haze of stars above her, feeling the crushed and fragrant grass beneath. Somewhere nearby a cricket chirped repeatedly. Loath to move and return to reality with all its doubt and questions, she lay still except for lips that pressed a kiss above the rhythmic thud of his heart.

She shivered a bit as her heated body cooled. Bjorn's arms tightened and he rubbed his chin against her hair.

"He's not the one for you, Skye," he said suddenly, his voice low and intense. "Don't go to him. Stay with us—with Karin."

His words dropped her back to reality, a cold contrast to the heat of their lovemaking. Without speaking, Skye pulled away from his arms.

Bjorn sat up and held out a hand. "Skye, what's wrong?"

She moved quickly out of reach. "This shouldn't have happened, Bjorn," she said, her voice tightly controlled. She pulled on her dress and tied the belt with shaking fingers.

"Why not? Because of Theo Brenner?" Bjorn growled, standing up and coming toward her. "He can't mean that much to you—not after the way you responded to me. Forget him, Skye," he said, pulling her into his arms. "You belong here now."

With a sudden, angry push, Skye freed herself. "I belong where I chose, Bjorn Stefansson." She turned and stumbled hastily through the dark toward the lake. Bess had returned and followed her.

"Skye! Wait a minute. Dammit, Skye, come back here!"

Skye fled along the water's edge guided by only the dim light of the moon, knowing she couldn't remain with Bjorn another second without breaking down completely. Tears streamed down her cheeks as she cut across the lawn to the back door.

The house was quiet, dark except for the upstairs hall light. Skye went quickly to her room and shut the door. Hugging her arms to her chest, she paced the floor, biting her lip in a vain attempt to stem the tide of tears.

For a few minutes tonight, she had been able to forget Bjorn's plan. She had been transfixed by her love for him, by the intensity of the feelings he aroused in her, new, exciting feelings that would have to be pushed aside again.

She heard him come into the house and froze, afraid he would come to her room and demand that she listen while he played through with his farce, perhaps add to the mockery with a proposal. Grabbing a nightgown, she went quickly across the hall to Karin's room.

As she leaned breathlessly against the door, she heard him come up the stairs and stop outside her room, knocking softly but insistently. She heard the door open and his muffled curse when he discovered the room was empty. Quickly she slipped on her nightgown and slid into Karin's bed. If he did check the room it would be unlikely that he'd risk waking his daughter.

Skye lay stiff, scarcely daring to breathe as the door slowly opened. From under her lashes, she could see his form in the doorway. He stood there for a long moment and she could feel his eyes on her.

"All right, Skye," he said finally, sounding weary. "We'll leave it for tonight—but tomorrow we talk. Good night." The door clicked shut.

Skye let out her breath and slowly relaxed. She hoped by tomorrow she would be back in control, able to handle whatever he had to say coolly and calmly. Moving closer to Karin, she gathered the sleeping child gently in her arms. While she could probably go back to her room without seeing Bjorn, it was comforting to hold the warm body close to her. She rested her cheek on the silky, sweet-smelling curls and closed her eyes.

Sleep did not come easily. Her body felt flushed and heavy, still lushly imprinted with the feel of Bjorn's, a sharp contrast to the turmoil of her thoughts.

She had run from Bjorn not wanting to hear the lies that were sure to follow, convinced that his lovemaking had been but another step toward the culmination of his plan to have her stay. Would he have gone so far as to propose marriage to her as he had suggested to Dave? Skye sighed softly. How determined was he about doing what he thought was the right thing for his daughter? She frowned, gazing into the dark corners of the room wondering if he would come to her again, and how much resistance she had.

Waking from a restless night, Skye went to her room just after dawn. She hurriedly dressed in cotton slacks and a T-shirt and went downstairs. Bess greeted Skye enthusiastically and they went out on the porch, into the cool, fresh light of a new day.

Skye knelt down and hugged the big dog, rubbing her cheek against the Newfoundland's soft black coat. "Well, Bess, old girl," she murmured. "Pretty soon it's going to be just me and you again." She bit her lip to keep back the sharp sting of tears. "Let's go for a walk."

They walked down to the lake. Sitting on the sand, Skye watched the sun climb steadily over the calm, silver surface, the dog pressed comfortingly against her side.

It was her birthday today. The year before at this time, she had been filled with a cautious but growing optimism for the future. How long would it be before she started to feel that way again?

She drew her legs up and rested her chin on her knees. It wasn't going to be easy to get through the birthday greetings and gift giving without revealing her inner anguish. It would be her last day with Bjorn and Karin. Tonight, after every one was asleep, she would leave. She knew it was a coward's way out, but it was the most painless way to escape.

She patted Bess's head. Escape—is that what leaving here was? She didn't feel trapped as she had with Reid. Indeed, she hadn't felt so wonderfully alive in years. If only Bjorn's love was real . . .

The dog pricked her ears and fanned the sand with a sweep of her tail. Without turning around, Skye knew, with a stab of dismay, that Bjorn had found her.

"Good morning," he said, sitting on the other side of the dog. "And happy birthday."

"Thank you," Skye murmured, her head slightly averted as she scooped up a handful of sand and let it trickle through her fingers.

"It's going to be another beautiful day," he said. "Just right for the barbecue Mary has planned." He looked at her, absently stroking the dog's head. "Skye—"

"I'd rather not talk about it," she interrupted quickly, knowing from the tone of his voice what was to follow.

"Why not?" he demanded harshly. "Maybe you felt it should never have happened, but you did nothing to stop me. Quite the contrary. If you think it was a mistake, okay. But I want to know why. Last night we were as intimate as two people can be. We should be able to talk about it."

"There is nothing to talk about," Skye said, keeping her voice calm and level. "It just happened, that's all. Let's just forget about it, shall we?"

"Maybe you can forget it that easily, but I can't." His voice was low and intense. "Dammit, Skye, I don't know what kind of...of relationship you had with your husband, or Brenner for that matter, but I thought what happened between us last night was—"

"Was the result of us being thrown together all summer," she interrupted. "A physical thing that happens sometimes between two healthy adults, that's all." She stood up and brushed the sand from her slacks. "I won't deny that I find you attractive, Bjorn, but that's as far as it goes," she lied.

He stood up slowly and looked at her, his face tight and controlled. "I see," he said finally. "Is it Brenner?"

"Yes," she lied steadily, then turned and walked away, feeling sick, knowing from the look on his face that she had convinced him. He would leave her alone, but the knowledge did not give her the relief she had expected. Instead she felt hollow, empty of all emotion except for dread of the lonely years ahead.

When Skye returned to the house Karin and Mary were awake and in the kitchen.

"Skye!" Karin looked up from her cereal and grinned excitedly. "Me an' Mary are going to bake your cake right after breakfast!"

"I can hardly wait to taste it," Skye said, giving her a hug before going to the cupboard for a coffee mug. "Don't go to any trouble, Mary," she said in an aside. "I'm not much for birthdays."

"A bit of a party will do you all some good," Mary said. "It's making Karin happy and—" She stopped and frowned worriedly. "Is everything all right between you and Bjorn?"

To Skye's dismay, she felt a rush of tears. Turning abruptly from Mary's gaze, she poured coffee into the mug, taking a deep breath to calm herself. "It's nothing to worry about," she said finally, managing a little smile as she sat down beside Karin.

Mary looked doubtful, obviously wanting to say more. "Well—okay. Would you like me to make you some toast?"

Skye shook her head. "No, thank you. I'm not hungry."

"I am," Karin piped up. "I finished all my cereal an' I'm still hungry." She held up her empty bowl. "Could I have some toast, please?"

"Of course you can, pet," Mary said with a fond smile.

Skye stirred her coffee slowly, staring into the steam that rose from the mug. This was the last morning she would spend like this, drinking coffee while Karin ate and Mary bustled about. She was going to miss the warm, homey atmosphere. Bjorn's house had always felt like home, she reflected, the home she had never had. Leaving was going to be so very hard.

As she raised her cup to her lips, Bjorn came through the door. For a second their eyes met, his cold, with a distance that hurt. She quickly looked away.

"Mary," he said, "I've got some running around to do this morning. I'll be back for a quick lunch and then I've got to go to the Shaws' and talk to Ian about the land he wants to rent from me. Don't worry, kiddo," he added, catching Karin's look of concern. "I'll be back in plenty of time for Skye's party."

Karin scrambled off her stool to stand beside him. "Make sure you don't forget, Daddy," she warned, looking up at him, her eyes serious. "Because you have to give Skye her present an' light the candles on the cake."

The final breakthrough had been made. Karin had openly acknowledged Bjorn as her father. His face was incredibly tender as he bent down to pick up his daughter.

"I won't forget, sweetheart," he said, hugging her close. "You make sure to help Mary while I'm gone."

"I will, Daddy." Karin pushed back, looking at him seriously for a minute and then solemnly kissed his cheek.

Bjorn hugged her again before putting her down carefully, his hand lingering to touch the tumble of chestnut curls. His eyes were misty when they met Skye's. "Thank you," he said huskily, and turned abruptly to leave.

"Well, thank God for that," Mary said quietly.

Skye could only nod as she blinked back tears. They'll be all right now, she thought. Even without me.

She swallowed the last of her coffee and stood up, forcing a bright smile.

"Well, I've got a couple of things to do myself," she said. "And I must get in to the bank today. Don't wait for me for lunch, Mary," she added, taking her cup to the sink. "If I'm late, I'll stop for something in town."

SKYE DROVE IN TO GIMLI feeling down and out but determined. She would leave tonight. There was nothing to be gained by staying. They would get along fine without her and she, in time, would learn to live without them.

She closed her bank account, getting traveler's checks for the trip ahead. She had the van filled with gas and the oil checked. Methodically finishing her business, she set about looking for one last thing.

Karin was going to miss both her and the dog. Skye wished she had the strength to leave Bess behind, but she knew she couldn't. Bess meant too much to her, and she would need her companionship.

She spotted a Kittens for Sale sign on a mailbox near one of the farms along the highway. Skye chose a tiny black kitten with a white nose and paws, cuddled it under her chin as she smiled her thanks at the children who sold it to her. She placed the cardboard box carefully on the floor of the van and drove off. She wouldn't give it to Karin outright, but would leave it for her along with a note that Bjorn could read to her.

Skye kept the kitten hidden in the van when she got back, knowing it would be safe and comfortable until she could safely sneak it up to her room.

"Where's Karin?" she asked Mary.

"With Bjorn," Mary explained. "He took her to the Shaws' with him. They have a little girl, Mandy, about the same age. Would you like some iced tea? I was just about to take a glass out to the patio.''

"I'll join you there in a few minutes," Skye said. "I have to go upstairs first."

She went quickly out the front door to her van and retrieved the box with the kitten, made a quick stop in the kitchen for a small dish, and hurried upstairs. A quick peek showed her the kitten was sleeping. She went to the bathroom and filled the disk with water then gently placed it beside the kitten. She tucked the big box out of sight and went to join Mary on the porch.

"How did the cake turn out?" she asked, sitting on a lounge chair and stretching out her legs.

"Beautifully, if I do say so myself. Karin left strict orders that you aren't to see it until after supper. Oh, and I'm to ask—how many candles?"

Skye laughed lightly. "Twenty-four. She's really enjoying this, isn't she?"

"Very much," Mary agreed. "She's come out of her shell a lot, Skye. You've been good for her."

"It's been mutual," Skye said, feeling a stab of pain at the thought of leaving—it would be a double loss.

When Bjorn and Karin returned, Karin was bubbling over with the excitement of having made a new friend and ran to tell Skye all about it.

"I was scared she wouldn't like me," she confessed. "But my daddy said of course she would. And I'm going to sleep over at her house maybe next week. She's got two beds—one for her and one for me. And you know what? She let me ride her bike even when I kept falling lots. But Daddy says he'll buy me a bike soon and I can practice."

Skye smiled, listening with pleasure as she chattered about her visit with Mandy. It was hard to believe this bright, happy girl was the same withdrawn child she'd pulled from the ice. Hoping fervently that her leaving wouldn't cause too much of a setback, she scooped the child into her arms, giving her a warm hug.

Bjorn came up behind them. "Let me in on that," he said, putting his arms around them.

Surprised, Skye stiffened and then relaxed, resting her head on his shoulder, warmed by the bittersweet touch. For those few seconds they were as Skye wished they could always be. She looked up to meet Bjorn's unreadable blue eyes, her lashes sweeping quickly down to hide her vulnerability. She felt his mouth move softly over her hair before he stepped back, giving Karin's cheek a pat.

"I'll go see if Mary wants the barbecue lit," he said, leaving them.

"He's a nice daddy," Karin confided. "I'm glad he's really mine."

"So am I, Karrie," Skye said, putting her down. "And I'm glad you have each other."

"Skye." Karin looked up at her solemnly. "You could stay and be the mother."

Skye's heart contracted with pain. "I can't stay, Karin," she said compassionately. "But I'll always be your friend. You know that, sweetheart."

Karin shook her head sadly. "But you won't be here."

There was nothing Skye could say. She stroked the child's curls and smiled with gentle sadness. "Let's go help Mary."

Karin's spirits climbed considerably when Mary had her tape balloons to one of the chairs around the patio table on the deck. She then put a birthday hat near each plate and ran to get the gaily wrapped presents to put beside Skye's chair.

"The steaks are ready, Mary," Bjorn called from the corner of the deck nearest the kitchen where the gas barbecue stood.

"So is everything here," Mary said, putting a tomato-and-cucumber salad on the table. "Let's eat."

Karin took Skye's hand and led her to the chair decorated with balloons. "You sit here at the head," she said. "In the birthday chair. Daddy, you sit beside Skye on one side, an' I'll sit beside her on the other side. Okay?"

"Okay with me, Karrie." Bjorn smiled at his daughter and set a platter on the table, taking his seat beside Skye.

Skye tried to be cheery, but it wasn't easy. Her throat was tight with emotion but she managed to smile and chat, pushing her food around on her plate in between tiny bites that she could hardly swallow.

Her masking of unhappiness was an all too familiar feeling. Had she really spent two years going through this with Reid, going through the motions of life, but hiding her true feelings?

She clapped and tried to show excitement when her birthday cake arrived with its blaze of candles. "Help me blow them out, Karin."

"Okay. Can I wish, too?"

"Of course you can."

"Is a wish a secret?" she asked.

"Only until it comes true," Bjorn answered.

Karin nodded, frowned thoughtfully for a moment and then leaned closer to the cake. "Okay, Skye. One, two, three—blow!"

After the cake had been cut and served, Karin excitedly handed Skye the presents one by one. Mary had teasingly given her a beginner's cookbook and a fine, ivory-colored shawl she had crocheted the winter before.

"It's beautiful, Mary," Skye said, stroking the soft wool. "Thank you. And," she added, picking up the cookbook with a smile, "if this starts with how to boil water, it'll be perfect!"

Karin's gift was a colorful ceramic butterfly broach. "Do you like it?" she asked anxiously. "It was my favorite one in the whole store."

"It's perfect," Skye said warmly. "And very pretty. Thank you very much. Can you pin it on for me, please?"

Karin carefully pinned the broach just below the collar of Skye's blouse, standing back for a moment to admire it. "Okay. Now Daddy."

Skye took the narrow package and opened it slowly. It was an oval-shaped silver locket. She laid it on the palm of her hand, tracing the delicate filigree around the edge.

"Look inside," Karin said excitedly.

Skye pressed the catch and opened the locket. Inside was a picture of Karin. It was a lovely, thoughtful gift and she felt her mask slip. "Thank you, Bjorn," she whispered, her eyes brimming with tears. "It's beautiful."

"Put it on for her, Daddy," Karin directed.

Bjorn put one hand on Skye's shoulder and turned her to face him as he leaned closer. She kept her eyes down as he took the locket from her and fumbled with the tiny clasp.

"Bend your head forward," he said, putting the locket around her neck and brushing her hair out of the way with gentle fingers. His warm breath stirred a wisp of hair against her cheek as he leaned closer to fasten the chain. "Are you still sure you want to leave?" he asked softly in her ear.

Startled, Skye pulled back and looked at him, but he merely smiled and straightened the locket, his fingers lightly tracing the chain above the swell of her breasts.

"It looks pretty," Karin declared with satisfaction. "Doesn't it, Mary?"

"It does indeed," Mary agreed. Her hazel eyes were thoughtful as she looked from Skye to Bjorn and back to Skye again. "Well, now—would anyone like more cake?"

After dinner Skye bathed Karin for the last time. They laughed together over soap bubbles Skye blew from the circle of her thumb and forefinger. Karin would wait for one to break free and then gleefully pop it with a slap of her hands.

"Come on, lovey," Skye said finally, holding out a big, fluffy towel. "Time to get into your jammies." She patted the wiggling body dry and rubbed the damp, curling hair, breathing deeply the fresh, soapy scent. She loved this little girl as her own. Karin would never replace Jennifer in her heart, but she had her own special place, easing Skye's pain and filling a void. She would miss her so much.

"What story do you want tonight?" Skye asked when Karin was tucked into bed.

"Umm—*Green Eggs 'n' Ham*."

Skye took the Dr. Seuss book from the shelf and sat on the bed, reading slowly. Karin chanted merrily along, her voice gradually becoming slower and broken by yawns. By the end of the book, she was snuggled under the covers blinking sleepily.

Skye turned out the light and bent down to kiss her. "Good night, sweetheart."

"G'night, Skye." Karin's eyes closed and then fluttered open again. "I wished . . . you were my mother," she murmured.

Skye blinked back tears and smiled sadly. "Sleep now, Karrie." She stroked her soft, round cheek. When the blue eyes drooped shut again, she quietly left the room, closing the door behind her.

"Karin asleep?" Bjorn asked over top of his newspaper when Skye returned to the living room.

Skye nodded as she sat down. "She was tired. It was a full day for her."

"You should have seen her with Mandy this afternoon." Bjorn broke into a smile. "They squealed and giggled—it would have driven me crazy if it hadn't been so great to see her acting like a normal, healthy child." He folded the paper and tossed it to one side, leaning forward in his chair, resting his arms on his knees. "Your being here has worked wonders, Skye," he said, his eyes intent on her. "Are you—"

"Here's Mary," Skye said, relieved at the interruption.

Bjorn sat silent while Mary chatted to Skye. Skye was conscious of his intense gaze, his expression still and brooding. She hated that look. She wanted to remember him with his eyes alight with laughter, a smile lurking in the lines on his face as he made some teasing comment. Unable to stand the tension she felt any longer, she made her excuses for an early night, going first to the kitchen to get some milk for the kitten.

Gently she lifted the kitten from its box noticing it had finished the water she'd left for it. Skye stuck her finger into the milk, letting the tiny, pink tongue rasp it clean. Soon, after much spitting and milk-muffled sneezes, it was drinking on its own. After it had finished, it tackled a wadded up piece of paper until, exhausted, it curled up on Skye's lap and slept.

Skye quietly packed while the rest of the house quietened. She heard Mary and then Bjorn come upstairs while she struggled to write a note to Karin. But nothing she wrote seemed to say what she wanted. Finally she gave up, wrote a simple goodbye and hoped that finding the kitten would be enough of a distraction for Karin.

Time passed slowly. The kitten woke up, drank some more milk and then played a rousing game of tail chase. Skye had to smile at its antics, glad she had thought of giving it to Karin. She was sure she'd love it.

When the kitten fell asleep again, she placed it gently back in the box and tiptoed quietly to Karin's room. Bess raised her head from the floor beside the bed and wagged her tail. Skye calmed her so she wouldn't bark, then put the box near the bed where Karin would be sure to see it as soon as she woke up.

She knelt beside the bed for a moment, gazing softly on the sleep-flushed face. Tears trembled in her eyes as she smoothed the tangle of silky curls for the last time. "Goodbye, sweetheart," she whispered and pressed a kiss on her baby-soft forehead. She lingered for a moment longer and then, dashing tears away with her fingers, signaled to the dog and they left the room.

She glanced down the hall toward Bjorn's room, tightened her lips grimly, and picked up her suitcases, slipping silently down the stairs, shadowed by the dog.

CHAPTER NINE

BRIGHT SILVER LIGHT reflected from the moon, spilling shadows across the lawn, giving an abstraction of daylight in a hundred hues of gray. Skye dropped her suitcases and stared around her, filled with an overwhelming sense of loss and loneliness. Tears ran hot down her cheeks and she leaned against the porch railing, closing her eyes against the pain. What was she doing?

She opened her eyes slowly and wiped the tears away with unsteady fingers. Why was she leaving? She loved Bjorn and she loved his daughter. They weren't asking her to leave—they wanted her to stay. If she left, there would be nothing for her but emotional emptiness. If she stayed, her life would be fuller, richer, happier— even without Bjorn's love.

She knew he didn't love her. She knew his prime motive for wanting her to stay was for Karin, but...he needed her. She remembered the night before and knew he wanted her. If she stayed, maybe someday he would come to love her.

BJORN'S ROOM WAS SOFTLY LIT by a beam of silver moonlight pouring through the open window and flowing onto the bed. He lay stretched out on his back, his head resting in the crook of one arm. The covers were flung over the lower half of his body and tangled in his legs. Skye went cautiously to the edge of the bed, her eyes moving from his shadowed face to the moongleam on his chest and over his taut, hard belly with its arrow of dark-gold curls. She touched her fingers to his shoulder.

His eyes opened instantly. "Who—" he muttered, his voice thick with sleep. "Skye?" He blinked sleepily. "What is it?"

"I—" Skye shook her head helplessly, lost for words.

Bjorn frowned and pulled himself into a sitting position. "What's wrong, Skye?" He took her hand in his and tugged gently, drawing her down to sit on the edge of the bed. "Tell me," he said, his eyes on her pale and stricken face.

Skye sat stiffly, nervously pleating the hem of her skirt. "I was leaving," she said finally.

"You mean now?" The sleepiness gone from his voice.

She nodded, still staring at her fingers.

"What about Karin?" he demanded. "Didn't you stop to think what your disappearance in the middle of the night would mean to her?"

Skye's heart sank. Karin. His first thought was always for his daughter. "I bought her a kitten," she said. "I thought it would help."

"You thought a pet would take your place? The kid looks on you like a *mother*, Skye!"

Tears streamed down her cheeks. "But I'm not her mother, am I?" She dashed a hand across her eyes. "What am I supposed to do—hang around until she's old enough to leave home?"

"If you really wanted to leave you would be gone by now," he said. "You're here and you're crying. That tells me you want to stay."

"What do you want, Bjorn?" she asked tensely.

"I want you to stay, of course. We all do."

She drew a deep breath. "In what capacity? As a companion for Karin or—"

"I want you to stay as the mother Karin needs—as my wife."

They were the words she had been expecting him to say ever since she had overheard his conversation with Dave. She wished they could bring joy. She looked at him, her eyes still and expressionless. "Bjorn I'll stay as . . . as your wife. On one condition."

"What?" The word was curt.

"No pretense." She shook her head emphatically. "I don't want any pretense about the reason for our marriage."

"I see. And what, may I ask, is that reason?"

"To give Karin a home, of course."

Bjorn stared at her silently, his eyes dark, pensive. "So the pretense you want to avoid is that we married for love," he said flatly.

"Yes," Skye said, her voice low as she stared at her hands. "I want honesty."

"All right, in the name of honesty, what about your relationship with Brenner? How does that enter into this?"

"Theo?" Skye looked up and blinked in surprise.

"Yeah. Your other . . . lover. Remember?" he asked harshly. "How do I know you won't go chasing off after him sooner or later?"

Skye cringed inwardly, discouraged by the heavy, sarcastic tone of his voice. "Theo and I are not lovers," she said carefully. "We're good friends, that's all."

Bjorn gave a derisive snort. "Tell me another one, sweetie. You made it pretty obvious what kind of friends you were."

"Dammit, Bjorn!" Skye there her hands up in frustration. "Do you really think I'm the kind of woman who would make love to one man one night and another the next?"

"I'm not sure what to make of you anymore, Skye," he said slowly. "I thought I knew—but now I'm not so sure." His eyes were brooding. "I had one wife who professed to love me—and left with another man. I'd be crazy to marry a woman who's already in love with someone else." His lips twitched bitterly. "What chance would there be?"

"Bjorn, I love Theo as a dear friend who quite literally saved my life. We are not and never have been lovers. We never will be." She looked at his deeply lined face, washed pale by moonlight. "It was all a lie," she added quietly.

"A lie?" He frowned. "Why?"

Skye drew a deep breath and plunged ahead. There was no reason to be dishonest. "Because of what I overheard you say to Dave."

Puzzled, Bjorn shook his head. "What did you hear? When?"

"The last morning at the Rosens'. You were sitting outside the bedroom where I was sleeping." Nervously she rubbed her hands together. "You were talking to him about Karin."

"I remember," Bjorn said slowly. "But what—"

"He said Karin would be upset by my leaving. And you said . . . you implied that you would consider marrying me to get me to stay."

Bjorn scowled. "And that made you fall into another man's arms? I don't get it."

Skye felt a flash of anger. "I understood only too well! All that . . . that romancing the night before! Why did you have to do that? Why couldn't you have just told me that you were worried?" She turned her back to him and hugged her arms to her chest. "Why did you have to pretend?" she whispered.

"Skye, tell me. How much of that conversation did you hear?"

"Enough," she said bitterly. "You were plotting to marry me because you wanted to keep me around for Karin."

"And what did Dave have to say about it?"

"He said it was a good idea, I think."

"He asked me a question—went straight to the heart of the matter. Did you hear it?"

Skye shook her head.

"He asked me, 'But do you love her?'" his voice was quiet. "Do you want to know what my answer was, Skye?"

Slowly she turned to look at him, her eyes wide and vulnerable.

"Yes," he said, his eyes intent on hers. "My answer was *yes*."

"Oh, Bjorn . . ." Her cheeks glistened with tears.

With a little groan, Bjorn pulled her to him, laying her head on his shoulder. "Don't cry, love," he murmured. "Tell me the rest."

Skye clung to his warmth. Her heart fluttered with hope. "I was hurt," she said finally. "That night—the dancing and all the rest—it had been so wonderful. I woke up feeling more alive than I ever had—"

"And then you overheard the wrong half of a conversation," Bjorn finished.

She nodded, her hair rubbing against his chin. "You hadn't paid that much attention to me before," she said. "At least not in…in a romantic way. To me your actions seemed to all fit as part of a plan to use me to make Karin happy, to ease your guilt." She sat up suddenly, pushing against his chest.

"Do you really love me, Bjorn?" she asked intensely. "*Really* love me? If you don't, let me know now. Please, don't lie."

"It's no lie," he said, taking her hands in his, his grip tight and reassuring. "I love you very much." He crooked a finger under her chin and raised her head. "Look at me," he whispered.

His eyes, with their glint of silver moonlight, held hers. "I love you, Skye Cameron," he repeated, the words softly impassioned.

Skye closed her eyes and let out a slow breath. "I—I might need some more convincing," she admitted, her lashes sweeping up again. "Just don't give up on me."

"Skye, am I to conclude from all this that you love me in return?"

"Of course. Isn't it obvious?"

"I need to hear it."

Skye leaned against him with a soft sigh, her hand stroking the side of his face. "I love you, Bjorn," she whispered shyly. "So very, very much." She pulled his head down and laid her mouth on his, her kiss sweet and giving.

His arms tightened around her and he returned her kiss fervently. Reluctantly he drew back, leaning against the headboard and closing his eyes. "One more thing,

Skye," he said. "I need to know about your husband."

"Reid?" Skye said with a note of surprise.

"Do you know that's the first time you've even mentioned his name to me? You've said absolutely nothing about him. Until Brenner arrived, I thought you were still in love with him."

"Never!" Skye stated with startling vehemence. "I hated him!"

Bjorn sat straight up and stared at her incredulously. "*Hated him!* But you wouldn't talk about him . . . you were still wearing his ring."

"The ring belonged to my mother," Skye said. "Reid's are somewhere on the floor of the Pacific Ocean. I threw them there after I left him."

"You left him? But—"

"I left him after Jennifer died." she interjected. "He died of a heart attack a few months later."

Bjorn shook his head in confusion, raking his fingers through his hair. "Start from the beginning," he urged. "Tell me the whole story."

Skye stared at their clasped hands, searching for words. "Reid was several years older than I was," she began finally. "My father's former partner in a law firm. He started courting me when I was eighteen. I had just started university. I had never dated much and he made it all seem so romantic—candlelight dinners, roses—all the trappings. I was so naive."

She told him about how cold and cruel Reid had been, of the fear and hate she had felt for him and about her flight after Jennifer's death. She told him of her meeting Theo and the strength his friendship had given her as she struggled to resume a normal life. Bjorn wrapped his arms around her and listened wordlessly, his embrace warm and comforting.

"I can't believe how wrong I got it all," he said with a shake of his head. "I'd even talked to Dave about you, asked him how long it might take you to get over things. He seemed to think that because you were still wearing your wedding ring, you still felt loyal to your husband, hadn't accepted the finality of his death." He shook his head again. "I was prepared to be patient, to give you the time you needed, and then I came back here to find Brenner waiting for you." He laughed shortly. "I'd never been jealous before, but I was burning with it, positive you were lovers. And then, to top it all off, you took the ring off. I thought you'd done it for him. Tied in with what Dave said, that made me feel sure you were ready to make a commitment to another man."

"I had put my mother's ring on when I went back to university. I guess I thought people would leave me alone if they thought I was married or...or widowed," Skye explained. "And then I fell in love with you. It just seemed silly to keep wearing it." She touched his shoulder lingeringly and smiled at him.

"I didn't know how closemouthed I was about everything," she said, "but it isn't easy to tell people that you hated your husband and were glad when he died. It took me a long time to realize that I had every right to feel as I did," she added, her eyes darkening with memory.

"Skye, were you a virgin when you married him?"

"Yes," she said quietly.

"What kind of lover was he?"

"Cold," she answered with a shudder she couldn't suppress. "Unfeeling—just as he was all the time.

"Did he ever hurt you?"

She looked down and nodded. "The first few times. But I got used to it."

Bjorn groaned and pulled her close to him, kissing her softly. "If I'd known," he said, his voice deep with contrition, "I would have been more gentle, considerate last night."

Skye shook her head. "All those times with Reid I felt used. His lovemaking was cold and calculated, so distant. I felt nothing and neither did he, not really. Last night was wonderful, so spontaneous. I could feel the passion, both in me and in you, Bjorn. It was exactly what I needed. You gave life to my body," she whispered against his lips. "And to my heart." She kissed him.

Bjorn's arms tightened and he held her close, returning her kiss slowly, thoroughly, then raised his head, his thumb stroking the nape of her neck. "Let me love you again," he whispered huskily. "Really love you this time, in my bed, with the moonlight gleaming on your skin and the whole night ahead of us." His lips met hers again.

Skye sighed, running her fingers over his chest down to where the sheet draped across his hips, lost to the magic of his kiss.

His fingers fumbled with the buttons on her blouse. "Let me undress you," he murmured.

With a shaky sigh, she pushed herself up, feeling the buttons give way. Her breasts thrust taut and full, anticipating his touch. As his hands brushed aside the material, he kissed each nipple lingeringly.

"Stand up," he whispered, unzipping the waistband of her skirt.

Skye stood up slowly, feeling the skirt fall around her ankles. She shrugged off the blouse, aware of his narrowed, desiring eyes, feeling passion mount quickly so that her legs felt weak and she wanted nothing more than to collapse onto him, to lose herself to his touch, to his love. She sank onto the bed, her lips parted and swollen with desire.

Bjorn kicked the sheet from his legs and pulled her into his arms. She stretched out beside him, her legs entwining with his, her breasts throbbing against his chest. As his lips covered hers, she moaned deep in her throat, pressing urgently against him.

He kissed her lips, then down over her neck, savoring her satin warmth and delicate scent. He kissed the pulse that fluttered in the hollow of her neck, cupping her breasts and fondling the thrusting peaks. He rolled to lie on top of her, stretching his legs over hers, so that his head lay cradled on her breasts and he could capture each nipple in turn, rolling, twisting, teasing with his lips.

Her every nerve quivered with a desire that grew with each caress of his hands and mouth. She needed him, needed this expression of their love. Her fingers curled in his hair and then moved to his shoulders, splaying over the rippling muscles of his back. "I need you, Bjorn," she whispered, her voice strained with need. "So very much. Make love to me."

He raised his head and smiled lovingly. "Soon," he promised huskily. "Soon, my love." He kissed her stomach, her thighs, moving down with hot, lingering kisses, his tongue touching, stroking, caressing until she curled her fingers in his hair and tugged with a moan. One hand skimmed over her hips, holding him to her as she gasped and arched against him.

"Bjorn . . . !"

He answered the plea in her voice with a quick turning move that brought him full length on top of her. His mouth closed over hers, answering her urgency with a thrust of his tongue and his hips, one startling burst of sensation. She moved with him, wanting, needing more, filling herself with his scent, his taste, his touch, his passion. Satiation was a consuming fire of need, of love . . . of rightness.

"SKYE?" he murmured later, lazily stroking her hip where it curved with his.

"Mmm?" She was drowsy with contentment and the newfound security of being loved.

"Will you marry me?"

She rubbed her cheek against his chest. "Yes."

He kissed her lightly. "Any conditions?"

"Just that you love me," she whispered. "That's all I ask."

His arms tightened and he kissed her deeply. "I do love you," he promised. "More than I ever thought I could love someone."

Tears welled in her eyes. "Oh, Bjorn, I feel so happy."

"Your happiness is all I want," he said gruffly. "I've seen too much sadness in your eyes."

"That was for Jennifer," she said softly.

"I know, love," he murmured with quiet sympathy. "Do you think you will want other children?"

"I—I think so. It will be scary, though. Actually," she added, touching her stomach lightly, "we might not have much choice in the matter. I wasn't exactly prepared for any of this."

Bjorn chuckled and hugged her. "Neither was I. I held myself back from you so much that when I did let go, I had nothing else on my mind." He moved his hands over her back and cupped her hips, pulling her to him.

"I need you in my life, Skye," he said intensely. "So much. Thank God you didn't leave."

"I couldn't leave, Bjorn," she whispered. "My life would have been unbearably empty without you. I love you so much." His mouth covered her ardently, and within minutes they were asleep.

Soon sunlight edged across her eyes and they flickered open. She stared for a moment at the unfamiliar room and then smiled. Rolling over, she nuzzled Bjorn's shoulder, breathing deeply, wanting to lie beside him forever. Reluctantly she began to inch her way to the side of the bed.

He stopped her. "Where are you going?" he asked sleepily.

"Back to my room," she said. "Before Karin and Mary get up."

"Uh-uh. You belong here now." One bare arm pressed her firmly against the mattress.

"But—"

"No buts." He nuzzled the warmth of her neck. "Karin will hardly notice and Mary will think it's about time."

"Well, at least let me pick up my clothes from the floor and put something on. I don't want to be too blatant."

"I like you naked," he said, cupping her breasts and rubbing his chin over the smooth skin.

"You're raspy," she complained mildly. The roughness was a new sensation and she pressed closer to him, running her hands over his back. "Have we got time?"

"For what?" His mouth closed over a thrusting nipple.

She gasped. "Making love again."

"You're insatiable."

"You started it."

"Mmm—let's finish it together."

"Then can I put something on?" she murmured, sliding down to press her body to his.

"As long as you don't make a habit of it. Hush now, darling. Kiss me."

They awoke again when the door flung open and Karin ran into the room, followed by the dog.

"Daddy! Look what I—" She stopped when she saw Skye. "Oh—I looked in your room already, Skye, and you weren't there. Look what I got!" She held up a squirming black-and-white bundle. "A kitten!"

Skye sat up, straightening the shirt of Bjorn's she had put on, sending him a rueful little glance. She didn't feel ready for this.

"Let's see, Karrie," Bjorn said, extending a lazy hand.

Karin carefully extracted the kitten's claws from her pajama sleeve and handed it to him, scrambling up onto the bed to sit between them.

Bjorn stroked the tiny animal with a gentle forefinger. "It's cute," he said. "It's a present from Skye, by the way, Karrie."

"Thanks, Skye." The child grinned happily.

"You're welcome. What are you going to name it?"

"Hmmm—Ginger!"

"Ginger?" Skye and Bjorn said together, looking at the black-and-white kitten.

"Yep. Mandy has a cat named Ginger. It's all kind of orange. Mandy says it's gold, but I don't think so." She took the kitten back from her father and snuggled it under her chin. "Skye—what are you doing in my daddy's bed?"

"You explain," Skye murmured dryly to Bjorn. "I wanted to leave—remember?"

Bjorn grinned lazily and propped himself up on one elbow. "Well, Karrie, last night Skye and I decided to get married. That means—"

"Skye's my mother?"

Bjorn smiled gently. "In a sense—yes."

Karin's eyes were round with pleased wonder. "That's what I wished when I blew on the candles. 'Member I told you, Skye?"

"Yes, sweetheart, I remember." Skye stroked the sleep-tumbled curls and kissed her tenderly. "I'm glad I'm staying."

"Me too." Karin sighed happily.

"Me three." Bjorn grinned.

"And Bessie four!" Karin shouted with a giggle as the dog laid her muzzle on the side of the bed and wagged her tail. "She wants up, too, Daddy."

"No way! Kids yes, kittens maybe, but I draw the line at colossal canines."

Karin giggled. "What does that mean?"

"No dogs," Bjorn answered, tousling her hair playfully.

"So this is where everyone is." Mary looked through the open door.

Skye ducked her head, blushing under the older woman's observant eyes, but Bjorn greeted her with cheerful aplomb.

"Morning, Mary," he said with a wide smile.

"Good morning. I take it congratulations are in order?" she drawled with a twinkle in her eyes.

"They are indeed, Mary. Skye and I are going to be married as soon as we can."

Mary smiled and nodded, obviously pleased. "I'm happy to hear that. You had me wondering for a while there. Come with me, Karin," she added. "I think we should celebrate this morning. You can help me make waffles."

"With strawberries," Karin said, sliding off the bed with the kitten.

"And back bacon," Bjorn said hopefully.

"And whipped cream." Skye grinned, her discomfiture gone.

"My, what a lot of hungry people there are around here this morning," Mary said dryly as she ushered Karin through the door and snapped her fingers at the dog to follow. She winked at Bjorn as she shut the door. "Breakfast in half an hour."

Bjorn shook his head as the door clicked shut. "Kids, cats, dogs and housekeepers! Tomorrow I buy a lock. No—don't get up yet," he instructed when she went to swing her legs out of bed. "Let's just lie here for a minute or two." He slid back down on the bed and pulled her into his arms.

Skye melted against him with a sigh of contentment, nuzzling his neck. "Do you know," she said after a minute, "I never spent the whole night with a man before. I think it could be habit-forming."

Bjorn pulled back and frowned. "Never? You mean—"

"He always left," she said with a grimace of distaste. "First to shower and then to his own room...as though I was...was unclean."

Bjorn's eyes were troubled. "Ah, love, I wish I could erase all the pain for you."

Skye smiled softly and stroked his cheek. "You have, Bjorn," she whispered with tender reassurance. "And replaced it with love."

He held her close, moved by the love he saw in her eyes. "I love you, Skye," he vowed. *"Always."*

**For the millions who can't read
Give the Gift of Literacy**

One out of five adults in North America
cannot read or write well enough
to fill out a job application
or understand the directions on a bottle of medicine.

**You can change all this by joining the fight
against illiteracy.**

For more information write to:
Contact, Box 81826, Lincoln, Neb. 68501
In the United States, call toll free: 800-228-3225

**The only degree you need
is a degree of caring**

"This ad made possible with the cooperation of the Coalition for Literacy and the Ad Council."
Give the Gift of Literacy Campaign is a project of the book and periodical industry,
in partnership with Telephone Pioneers of America.

LIT—A.—1

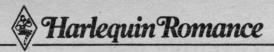 **Harlequin Romance**

Coming Next Month

Available in July wherever paperback books are sold, or through Harlequin Reader Service.

In the U.S.
901 Fuhrmann Blvd.
P.O. Box 1397
Buffalo, N.Y. 14240-1397

In Canada
P.O. Box 603
Fort Erie, Ontario
L2A 5X3

ATTRACTIVE, SPACE SAVING BOOK RACK

Display your most prized novels on this handsome and sturdy book rack. The hand-rubbed walnut finish will blend into your library decor with quiet elegance, providing a practical organizer for your favorite hard-or soft-covered books.

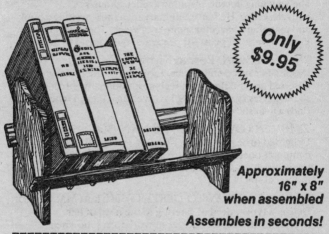

Only $9.95

Approximately 16" x 8" when assembled

Assembles in seconds!

To order, rush your name, address and zip code, along with a check or money order for $10.70* ($9.95 plus 75¢ postage and handling) payable to *Harlequin Reader Service*:

Harlequin Reader Service
Book Rack Offer
901 Fuhrmann Blvd.
P.O. Box 1325
Buffalo, NY 14269-1325

Offer not available in Canada.

BKR-1R

*New York residents add appropriate sales tax.